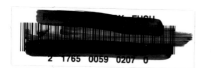

NEW DIRECTIONS 28

New Directions in Prose and Poetry 28

Edited by J. Laughlin

with Peter Glassgold and Frederick R. Martin

 A New Directions Book

Copyright © 1974 by New Directions Publishing Corporation
Library of Congress Catalog Card Number: 37–1751 (Serial)

ACKNOWLEDGMENTS

Grateful acknowledgment is made to the editors and publishers of books and magazines where some of the selections in this volume first appeared: for Walter Abish (Copyright © 1973 by Walter Abish), *The Element, Extentions,* and *TriQuarterly;* for Ernesto Cardenal, The Johns Hopkins University Press (published in Spanish as *Homenaje a los indios americanos,* Copyright © 1970 by Editorial Universitaria, S. A.; translation Copyright © 1973 by The Johns Hopkins University Press); for William Everson, Cayucos Books (Copyright © 1973 by William Everson); for James Purdy (Copyright © 1973 by James Purdy), *Antaeus* and *Esquire;* for Carl Rakosi, *New Letters* (Copyright © 1973 by The Curators of the University of Missouri) and *Quadrant* (Australia); for Roberto Sanesi, *Antaeus* (Copyright © 1973 by *Antaeus*).

Manufactured in the United States of America
First published clothbound (ISBN: 0–8112–0525–8) and as
New Directions Paperbook 371 (ISBN: 0–8112–0526–6) in 1974
Published simultaneously in Canada by McClelland & Stewart, Ltd.

New Directions Books are published for James Laughlin
by New Directions Publishing Corporation,
333 Sixth Avenue, New York 10014

CONTENTS

MINDS MEET

WALTER ABISH

A History

The Chappe brothers were skilled technicians, and as such their aspirations were confined to the realization of their undertaking. They had never traveled to the heart of Mexico, and there climbed the broad steep steps of the massive Mayan, Toltec, and Aztec pyramids which constituted an altogether different system of communication from the one they were exploring. In France the Chappe brothers worked around the clock perfecting the semaphore. One at a time they worked the arm that was attached to an upright mast on the roof of their house. In those days the roofs were slanted, and working the arm at night was extremely hazardous. In a later version, also perfected by the Chappe brothers, the arm was equipped with two mobile extensions, and in this form 192 signals could be sent simultaneously, although 192 signals was a bit much for a man to absorb at one time.

The Chappe brothers felt exhilarated when the French government under Napoleon requested that they transmit to the Dutch the following message: Is there any other way to live? Justifiably, the three brothers felt that they were making headway. It is not known what the Dutch made of the message, since they never responded to it. According to the 23rd edition of the *Encyclopedia of the U.S.S.R.*, S.F.B. Morse, an American portrait painter, was

1

inspired to invent the Morse code after seeing an illustration of one of Chappe's semaphores in action during the siege of Conde-sur-l'Escaut, in November 1794. The illustration showed some soldiers bivouacked in a meadow a short distance from a three-story square tower that was situated on the slope of a low hill. The wood ramp and railing on the tower enabled the signal man to work the semaphore arm mounted on the roof. By no stretch of the imagination could these towers be compared to the imposing edifices built by the Pre-Columbians, but they were functional, they served a purpose, and they were inexpensive. The United States installed some in Connecticut in 1802, others along the coast of Maine in 1807, and by 1832, a network of considerable length linked Washington to the other cities in the East. Still, the most ambitious system by far was erected under Nicholas I (1825–52) when his government built stone towers at a distance of four to five miles apart, connecting St. Petersburg to Moscow. Nicholas eventually hoped to build a chain of towers to the Bering Strait, into Canada by way of Alaska, then down the west coast of the U.S. to Mexico, to the heart of the ancient empire, to the pyramids, those crumbling overgrown ruins that at one time had been Mayan signal towers, something that most archeologists had clearly failed to realize. Nicholas, at heart a resourceful romantic, wanted to plug into the Pre-Columbian system, though it is doubtful to this day whether he could pronounce the word "Tlahuizcalpentecutli," which in the Mayan language means, "Lord of the Dawn." At any rate, Nicholas's colossal undertaking can be said to rival that of Montezuma II, who prior to the arrival of Cortes was determined to discover "that which must come," only to have his astrologers, court sorcerers, and the thousands who came to the palace with their dreams put to death, because their forecasts were unacceptable.

After Nicholas's death, his son dutifully continued to pay for the upkeep and maintenance of the signal towers, although most of the messages that came pouring in from the ancient Mayans were not transmitted to Moscow, since vital sections of the line in the U.S. found it more profitable to switch to commercial messages. In some instances, subscribers were paying upward of $85 a month to be informed of a ship's arrival from Europe. As a result of this quite a number of signal men made a tidy packet and retired early. It must also be said that the majority of the signal men were Russians, which posed a problem for the U.S. Signal Corps, because the diet of the Russians was so different. Anyway, S.F.B. Morse once climbed a Mayan pyramid to get a better understanding of the system. Reaching the top he heard a babble of voices, as 3,000 years of incomprehensible history pressed down on him. Undaunted by the noise, he told the voices "to piss off." He was not concerned with history, or with the Aztec "Law of the Center." Five years later, while teaching at N.Y.U. he copied the famous experiment of Abbe Nollet, a Carthusian monk who was able to transmit an electric charge over a mile-long line of monks "who leaped simultaneously into the air and laughed heartily afterward." S.F.B. Morse, no sluggard where electricity was concerned, had the U.S. government round up all the Russian signal men, then, having handcuffed them to one another, kept them jumping for forty-eight hours. It was not a solution in communication . . . at least not for some years to come.

To this day the Mayan files are collecting dust in the archive in Moscow. An attempt had been made to translate them, and the first sentence reads: Is there any other way to live? But the Czar soon lost interest in the project, although he continued to pay for it. Some of the signal towers are still inhabited; however, only one near Dublin has received any attention in the press.

A Message

There are twenty-six letters in the alphabet. The first letter, A, resembles the twenty-second letter, V. It has a crossbar that links the two converging straight lines halfway between their ends and the point where they meet, and resembles an arrowhead pointing straight upward. The letter V, which does not have a crossbar, points in the opposite direction. Even someone unaccustomed to the alphabet will have no difficulty in distinguishing the one from the other. Arrowheads are not extinct as one might suspect. They are still painted on all sorts of directional signs, i.e., This way to the abyss, or simply MENS ROOM.

In spite of the undeniable resemblance, a person pierced by an arrow does not think of the letters A or V. In general, people are conditioned to think of altogether different things. Most likely in the U.S. and in other places where Western Civilization has taken a stranglehold, people think of more immediate things. They think of Errol Flynn, or Wilhelm Fürtwangler.

In some of the more backward areas in the Southwest people still use arrows. Disdainfully they shoot them into deer, and moose, and bears. In parts of New Mexico the plains are littered with arrowheads . . . From the air the ground looks like a giant alphabet soup.

The sky darkens gradually, but in spots the night sky remains brightly lit as more and more buildings go up in flames. Surprisingly no one shows any apprehension at this frequent occurrence. It is being taken for granted the way one person after another collapsing behind the checkout counter of your local supermarket from an excess of toxicity is taken for granted. Although the letters of the alphabet are independent of each other, people tend to ingest or read them, as the case may be, in small and large clusters that are called words. No matter what people say to each other, they are using words, not letters. When a word is not understood, the person using it is obliged to spell it aloud. This entails breaking the word into letters. However, if one is careful, one can speak for hours on end, even months sometimes, without once being compelled to spell a word . . . In the more rural sections of the U.S. people do not resort to spelling difficult words . . . instead they plunge a V-shaped knife into the other fella, who moans, "Ohhh." O also happens to be the fifteenth letter in the alphabet. For some reason it is often used by insecure people.

In the larger cities man's literacy is generally taken for granted. When an alarm goes out, the recipient will write on a card the location of the reported fire. The firemen are notified, and, having slid down from their living quarters on a greased pole, gather round the large wall map of their district to discuss the best approach. Many of the streets are blocked . . . many of the street signs missing . . . or pointing in the wrong direction. Still, the map is of some help. It gives the firemen a decided advantage. For one thing, all the street names are printed on the map. When a street is no longer being used, the street name is crossed out on the map. For that purpose an X, or several X's may be used. X is also the twenty-fourth letter in the alphabet. No one ever moans X, or exhales X. Only coy women will say: Although everything is predetermined, X baffled me last night.

Many couples communicate with each other by leaving notes on the kitchen table. Harry comes home and reads what his wife has written. Most notes are expressly reserved for factual if somewhat prosaic statements: I have gone away, you will never see me again. The casserole should be heated at three-fifty for half an hour. If Harry feels like it he will also write a note. On reading a note it should be possible to discover if the person writing it harbors ill feelings toward one. Frequently, for one reason or another, the author of a note may try to disguise his or her ill feelings, but like most things kept bottled up, ill feelings will out. If not in this note then surely in the next.

It is also customary for people to sign the note with their own names. They write Harry or Joe, or just initial it, H or J . . . to let the person for whom the note is intended know that they and not someone else has written it. Not infrequently the writer of notes will feel impelled to address a larger audience. He may, on his way home, stop at one of the public conveniences in the subway and write in capital letters above the urinal: Does the past leave any room for the future? The writer will have the satisfaction of knowing that many men will ponder over this question as they stand with legs apart on the brink of an incertitude that nothing will relieve.

Harry was embracing his wife when the message arrived. But they were no longer together by the time the message was deciphered a few years later. They were still avidly reading notes left for them on the kitchen table. These notes, respectively signed Bruno and Tina, helped somewhat to diminish their disquietening sense of apartness. Energetically Harry, with a compressed feeling of anguish, clipped all the articles dealing with the message from the local paper. It enabled him to recall the precise moment the message was received. To situate the exact location of their embrace, Harry tried to remember the interior of their former apartment, and while drawing its floor plan he discovered that it resembled the floor plan of his present apartment. What to do, he wondered.

In the building where Harry works, people dislike using the elevator. Quite candidly they admit to being afraid . . . As they shoot up to the thirty-third floor they shout obscenities at the operator. But all this anger does not alleviate the terror. Many unaccountably spend long hours holding their throbbing heads between their hands and crouching in a retching position. Afterward they say:

tough shit. The message did nothing to assuage people's longing and desire to come together. Harry stretched out on a mat and dreamt of impromptu sex. Now, he whispered, this second, I am ready and waiting for you. But no one rang the bell. By the time Tina entered the room ten minutes later, it was too late, decidedly too late.

Of the many divisions in the army only one is called the Big A. The men in it wear green fatigues just as the men do in the other divisions. The Big A is chiefly a useful administrative label. It is one way of having the Chiefs of Staff organize the defense of the President on paper without being plagued by tedious duplications. It also makes it possible to send one regiment to relieve another at the White House, or dig ditches for sewers . . . or do something else that is constructive.

The men of the Big A can be distinguished by their colorful shoulder patch which shows a big A on a blue background with a gold border. It's nothing fancy. There is no howling hyena on a volcano, just the letter A. The men seem to be satisfied. The patch is in the shape of a shield. The green fatigues the men wear cancel and reject all parallels that may be drawn to the age of chivalry.

The soldiers have their urinals and their beds. There is a general sort of rhythm to their everyday existence. Some have wives, others keep the names of available girls in spiral notebooks. Their needs, in other words, are taken care of. The shoulder patch unites them in a way. The letter A in this instance remains a situation. It may, for a historian who studies these matters of the heart, be a hopeless one, but how else can one keep the forest from moving in . . . how else can one prevent the stark and forbidding mountains from encroaching upon desolate cities. With a studied air of diffidence the soldiers read the message: Is there any other way to live? Over and over again.

Taken Aback by the Message

Harry discovers Gwen in bed with Tobias and is taken aback. He says to himself, I am taken aback. His face more or less confirms this. Dubiously he inspects his face in the bathroom mirror. He is filled with a profound melancholy as well as distrust. How confusing, he thinks. Do I mistrust my melancholy, or am I melancholy because I am riddled with mistrust.

Most men feel frustrated by the time they reach thirty because there are only so many ways of making love. While the lower part of the body is actively engaged during this act of passion the face questions the veracity of its own existence. In its distress it beams all kinds of signals to the other face. These signals are by no means reliable. One might say that the faces are immersed in the self.

Tobias is a health freak. He restricts his intake of carbohydrates and teaches history at night school. It leaves him a lot of time during the day. He and Gwen share in common a love for history. He is expounding on the failure of the New Deal, while she is holding his limp prick. Harry is in five places at the same time. He is at the keyhole, in the stairwell, in the basement, passing in a bus, at work . . . Over the years his emotions have been eroded. Yet Gwen is the first to agree that Tobias is a fraud, but that doesn't prevent her from reviving his limp prick. I have discarded emotions, Tobias told her during their thirteenth bout. Emotions do not replenish me.

Harry is incensed. Losing his wife Jane, then Tina, and now Gwen to Tobias is a negligible matter compared to the deliberate assault by Tobias on his emotions. Harry stares searchingly at himself in the mirror. He is beginning to look more and more like Tobias. He strokes his new mustache and carefully straightens the black wig he is wearing. Tuesday he plans to invest in a pair of shoes with hidden lifts which will make him at least two inches taller. In this manner, he too hopes to discard emotions, and become a successful historian.

The Abandoned Message

Two million eight hundred and thirty-three thousand vehicles were abandoned in the countryside during the first quarter of this year. A sizable number of the abandoned cars contained people . . . some also contained pets. Of course, by the time a car is found it has already been stripped of its engine, its tires, and anything else that may be useful to another driver. In most cases the cars had run out of gas, and the driver, passengers, and pets, out of luck. Unwilling to abandon the car many people heroically stay with it.

Technically, as long as they remain in the car, the car cannot be considered abandoned. At one time the film industry exploited the theme of abandonment. It went to great length to build up the myth of the abandoned husband. Although some of these films were made over thirty years ago they can still be seen on television. Generally the movie's climax, if it can be called that, is reached when the wife, returning from her millionaire lover, drives her Rolls over the body of her missing husband. Bewildered they stare at each other. She accompanies him to the hospital, abandoning her car. It is not too painful, he assures her, as millions of married men bite back their tears, and their wives, in panic at their husbands' distress, welcome the oblivion into which they have sunk. Still, the word "abandoned" is rarely used in the film. In actual life it is used all too frequently; i.e., we should abandon Harlem, or we abandoned our children. Abandoned children grow up to make love like other people. But there is a sadness, a lingering wet sadness on their sallow faces as they pick up a girl on the road, and then drive their cars in circles until they have run out of gas.

To Gwen the word "abandon" is nothing new. She's familiar with the story of the abandoned little girl. Swept away by the tremendous pathos of the story, she accuses her father of turning her out. You slammed the door in my face. It was ice cold winter and you abandoned me. All I had to keep warm was a box of matches. Harry is disturbed whenever Gwen's father comes to visit, comes to plead for forgiveness. She lets him caress her small pointed breasts. His tears leave moist spots on her freshly starched dress. He's a bit daft, she tells Harry. He still thinks I am fourteen.

What are you planning to do this morning? asked Harry.

I am going to love myself and remember things . . .

As things stand there is a residue of bitterness about the message. Harry equivocates, he can't decide whether or not the 1,000-foot metal reflector at the Arecibo Ionospheric Observatory should have been destroyed. It took eight years to assemble and will take at least five years to repair. Most of the scientists were evacuated by boat to St. John in the Virgin Islands, where they spend their time drinking duty-free liquor, and making tooled leather belts. Their happy frame of mind is causing a lot of people to have second thoughts about the future destruction of scientific equipment.

Harry, sitting in his room, thoughtfully says: I can't think of anyone to abandon.

Abased by the Message

Some women are known to leave their apartments not later than ten each morning. They are the furtive recipients of a message. This is written all over their flushed but inscrutable faces. But no one can make out the message itself. Gwen takes a taxi to her destination. She feels quite relaxed, and even strikes up a conversation with the driver, who confesses that he has been driving past her building for the last two weeks, hoping that she would hail his cab. Nothing can undermine her confidence. She stares at the back of his large closely cropped head, and reads his unpronounceable name on the dashboard. All things being equal, she gives him a large tip, as well as her telephone number. She is sometimes given to impulsive behavior. In less than an hour she will be sipping coffee and describing her totally irresponsible action. She likes to hear herself speak. She likes to be surprised by her own words. It is spring or summer as she races up the two flights of stairs and embraces whoever answers the door. Of course, things do not always go according to plan. There's that initial awkwardness that has to be overcome, when the man keeps repeating: But who are you? What do you want? After further delays and hesitations, the man panics and locks himself in the bathroom. No amount of pounding on the door will make him open it. All this care on what to wear is thrown to the wind, Gwen tells Harry. But the next time I'll come prepared, I'll put it in print, and slip it under his door.

Abasement is located in the mind, but sometimes it is performed for the benefit of the heart. Gwen pictures herself lying in bed with the two-hundred-pound taxi driver she met the day before. I am totally independent, she says to herself. In spring or summer a woman carefully examines the moist stains on her white dress, gladly accepting a handkerchief from the first man she meets, fully aware of his complicity. I want to experience my distress in every which way, says Gwen. The stains are washed out in lukewarm water. The distress on the woman's face is only temporary. It appears to be related to the stains on her dress.

Harry reluctantly listens to Gwen describe her most recent abasement. It resembles Irma's in Tripoli. What did you do when the two-hundred-pound taxi driver followed you into the building? Gwen grimly describes the situation. Their conversation is studded with technical terms. Harry feels restless. He lights a cigarette. He opens a window. He paces up and down the room. Theoretically at least half of the room is his. But which half. Left or right?

Abashed While Receiving the Message

Harry is intensely sensitive to what others think of him. He is so afraid of asking the wrong question, or mispronouncing a word, that frequently he gets on a bus and rides all the way to the end of the line rather than ask the driver or one of the passengers where the bus is going. Many men, like Harry, are not certain what day of the week it is. Yet others have minds like clocks.

Harry steps into a bank in Queens and points a pistol at the bank teller. Let's have all your dough, he says. Dough, mocks the teller. What do you think this is, a bakery? Next thing you'll be asking for bread. Harry blushes furiously. He is being mocked. He feels abashed. It is a familiar quandary, so he shoots the bank teller, and then hops on the first passing bus outside the bank. Killing is a stabilizing factor in this society. But in no time Harry is again filled with a familiar panic, he doesn't know in which direction the bus is headed.

Harry undresses a woman and then undresses himself. He prolongs the undressing; he folds his trousers, his shirt, his handkerchief. He is relieved that the woman is not his wife Jane, or Tina, or Gwen, or Irma. She is someone he will not run into again. The woman cannot resist laughing when she notices the tattoo of the Mysterious Lady over his heart. Harry sees nothing funny about the tattoo. Beds also act as stabilizing factors, but not tattoos. She is still laughing when he leaves her room half an hour later. Problems between couples frequently arise . . . I'm too modest, thinks Harry bitterly, and there are gaps in my memory. I no longer remember where I met the mysterious woman of my heart.

Once the Knowledge of the Message Has Abated

When a knife is pulled out of the body, the pain is said to have abated . . . although dying, too, is a form of abatement. People have a predilection for the tangible. They rest on beds, on chairs, on tree stumps, on walking sticks. Napoleon once observed that people cannot rest comfortably on their bayonets. But this remark has been taken out of context. It was lifted from a letter Napoleon wrote to his brother-in-law who had a lot of unruly people on his bayonets in Poland. In any event, where there is no room for stress, for love, for anger, there is even less room for abatement.

People everywhere study the calendar, and mark each day as it passes into a funereal darkness, out of which the next day emerges. They mark their birthdays on their calendars, and skip certain days to bring the moment of their happiness closer. The calendar is standardized . . . and no matter how one looks at it, it is a measure that encloses the apartness with all its offensive sounds. Last year on that and that day I met so and so, a woman will say to herself. I was alone as I am now . . . I smiled at him . . . I was wearing my see-through dress. My breasts were beaming messages to his eyes. Memories are also stabilizing factors. They preserve and restore as well as animate. Why else would one wish to plunder the museums? Still, memories in their random selectiveness can be said to perform a kind of abatement.

But as far as color is concerned, memory remains about as reliable as black-and-white film. Harry studiously examines the photographs of a nude at the Museum of Modern Art. He has lost all sense of time. He finds the nude engrossing, most attractive, incredibly provocative. The nude stares back at him. The museum is empty, the gates are locked, the lights are out. Somewhere in the building a guard is inserting his passkey into all kinds of elaborate electronic devices. There may even be an alert German shepherd at his heels. If all this is true, thinks Harry, then why hasn't my mind triggered the alarm system? Can it be that my mind doesn't exist?

The Abbreviated Message

When the Chinese Communist Forces wish to pass for the Cooperative Commonwealth Federation, or when a physician wishes to convert his patient's conditioned reflex into a critical ratio, they abbreviate. When the dead are picked up and brought to the assembly area it is aways on CR, carrier's risk. People have been known to lose an arm or leg in transit. They are dw. Deadweight, not dustwrappers. How easy it is to shift from the intensity of one's inclination which is abbreviated "I," to the moment of inertia, by simply leaving the letter "I" untouched.

The Aberrant Messenger

The bus driver presses down on the accelerator and crashes through the barricades. At night his wife Nora waits for him in bed, while he, bare-chested, smokes cigarette after cigarette. She trusts him because he is quick to respond to the insults that are heaped on her each day. She can't wait to tell him about it when he comes home. On his day off he accompanies her to the supermarket, to the drive-in bank, the swimming pool, the hairdressing salon, the bowling alley, his face flushed with indignation as she is being insulted . . .

At the motor pool he greets his friends. He's lost a lot of weight since his wife started to complain that she was being insulted. If he had not come from a poor home, he would have studied archeology, or some similar discipline. While the message is being deciphered, the bus drivers chat about their daily run. There's a grim sort of know-how in the way they lean against their buses as they wait for the word to come from Arecibo. All over the United States, bus drivers are practicing the rapid loading and unloading of their passengers. Harry passes his driving test, but the inspector is skeptical about the American flag tattooed on his hand. It looks too new.

Harry follows Nora at a safe distance. She reminds him of a bus . . . the iridescent longing on his face arouses in Nora a feeling of palpitating disgust. She waits for him at the entrance to the building. She waits for him to insult her. She invites him up to her apartment. They stand like two archaic sculptures in the room, each ready to fall at the slightest shove. I detest your hair, your nose, your caved-in chest, says Nora. But you're looking at me upside down, protests Harry. Oh, she says.

The mountains are closing in on the city . . . everyone furtively examines the pavement each day to see if it is beginning to crack. There is no way of verifying the message. It will take upward of two thousand years to receive a reply. I've slept with Jane, I've slept with Gwen, I've slept with Irma, and now I've slept with Nora, ponders Harry.

The Message Kept in Abeyance

When an unprecedented number, three thousand, men and women plunge into a water hole in Arkansas and discover a rhino in their midst, their purpose is said to be temporarily in abeyance. In this society love slips away the moment the mail is not promptly delivered. The mailmen are past masters at this . . . they also open all the third- and fourth-class mail. They gorge themselves on manuscripts and unsolicited photographs of American Indians. By the time they get home they are saturated. Even their brains begin to reek of glue.

Nora likes to send postcards to her friends whenever she's on vacation. A restlessness drives her to seek out the Rockies. She's not afraid of earthquakes, floods, or tornadoes, since she spends the greater part of each day sheltered in the arms of the local mailman, who confides to her his bleak vision . . . and leaves her on the last day with the suggestion that she stay another week, because his friends on the night shift would like to meet her.

Everywhere people wind their watches to postpone the abeyance that threatens to overtake them. One sharpshooter on a tower can paralyze the traffic for hours. Once a bullet has entered the body, it's best to contemplate the past and not the future. The present can be said to be in a state of painful abeyance.

The Message Is Abhorrent

It can happen on any occasion: for instance, when visiting a friend just as he's about to garrotte his wife. To avoid the abhorrent, one must resist the persistent invitations from habitual murderers, and from people who hang outlandish looking weapons on the crimson-colored walls of the dining room.

To map the abhorrent simply follow the shrill shrieks for help. It's best to keep a pencil and a piece of paper handy. One man went down a sewer to recover his leg, only to discover that it wasn't his.

With the construction of the Great Chinese Wall, travel as we know it came to a virtual standstill. The Great Wall impeded movement . . . People resisted being walled in. They complained that their imagination was being stifled. Pole vaulting became a national pastime . . . What are we dividing with our walls, mused Harry.

We are dividing our abhorrence. Soon, as more and more walls are added, our present abhorrence will survive only as a faint memory.

What do you look like, people shout at each other across the walls. They lie about their appearance. It is pointless, really, but pole vaulting has left its scars. Their bodies follow an arc of ninety degrees in the air as they practice vaulting over the wall. No one has yet succeeded. Half the men in this country are bricklayers, the other half are dying from exhaustion. But Harry is well out of it. He has summed up his present position, but once the abhorrent has been eradicated, he plans to sum it up again.

I don't like the way you swallow your words, says Jane. I don't like the way you try to disguise your weakness by growing long sideburns, or the way you use an entire page when you sign your name in the hotel register . . . and I'm not crazy about the headstone you picked for me.

The Ability to Read the Message

To slide open the window and let in the cold air is to initiate an action with irreversible results. As the mind relinquishes the visual implosion, the brain cells rush items of urgent information back and forth in blind haste . . . a kind of paralysis sets in. Intention is frozen in incertitude. People are confident that they control the opening and closing of their windows . . . it imbues them with a misleading certitude that is bound to have widespread repercussions. Men think nothing of it when at night their wives ask them to shut the window. Naked they jump out of bed . . . some never make it to the window . . . some never make it back . . . Who is to measure the perils that one may encounter between bed and the opening, that rectangular opening in the wall.

A measure of man's need to survive is to be found in his pressing need for windows. Brimming over with self-confidence he stands at the window courting disaster. The man who opens other people's windows is afraid that if he would use the door he might be asked to stay for dinner. Entering through the window is an assault . . . Even though the people who live in that house or apartment may be starved for affection, they would never dare embrace the man who has soiled their linen with his boots.

Ability is a mountaintop to which people cling . . . in order to breathe the pure air, in order to give their lungs a change of pace. I'm unable to decide between him or her, says the ventriloquist. Their moans are so alike . . . but not the freshly painted windows in their room. I'm sick to death of filling puppets with voices of doom.

The Message Above

The above is chiefly referred to by people who are familiar with the below. The skywriter, like you and me, enjoys an occasional chat with his neighbor's wife. In marked contrast, horses and collectors of rare china weave back and forth with delicate, almost prissy motions. Their exercises show a kind of refinement, a result of inbreeding . . . Horses are kept in houses that are called stables, and mostly, with rare exceptions, breed only with their own kind. Collectors channel their furious energy into collecting . . . they have been known to abstain from sexual intercourse out of a desire not to spread their beautiful glaze.

When a pilot flies upside down, the above seeks to pull him below. The subject of the above is broached in most of the literature of the antiquities. It has also marked the American sensibility. I'm not above sleeping with my friend's wife, Tobias tells Harry. In Minnesota twenty thousand people gathered in the main square and watched Tobias as he demonstrated the toy helicopter. Hallelujah, they cried, as he stayed aloft for over two hours.

The Message Is Absent

The messenger wears a clean shirt, but the grime is visible under his nails . . . The sky is a dull grey, but farther out, only a few hundred miles away, it is a Mediterranean blue. Everyone evokes its blue absence . . . People indiscriminately speak about each other's tragedies . . . they speak about them in an almost flippant manner so as not to be carried away by the imminence of the startling discovery that they are totally immune to the burning house next door, and have no further need to disguise their diffidence. So the absent is a solution . . . If the house next door is not burning, so much the better . . . The messenger spotted the two men in leather jackets waiting for him in the hallway. He stopped. He hesitated. He raced back upstairs, they in hot pursuit. He ran past the doors, the closed doors with the familiar numbers: 5a, 5b, 5c, 5d, 6a, 6b, 6c, 6d, 7a . . . but there was no seventh floor. Everything that is not here is absent. The only thing that is not absent, said the policeman's wife, is lust. May I, asked the messenger, unbuttoning her blouse. He had a clean shirt on, she said afterward, justifying her amorous response, a response that had been all out of proportion to his.

In this humdrum life so many encounters lack the specificity of a stain. Everywhere the housewife looks there is lust staring back at her. It is cold clinical lust, compressed into a can of shaving soap. She stares at it fixedly. One day she will cover herself with it.

The dockworkers assemble each day at the pier. They say "present" when their names are called. They all have strong emotional fathers . . . They have daughters who have learned to say: That's wonderful to hear. The men are unpacking crates that contain machinery from Japan. The message on their muscles bulges with a fierce hunger, an unreliable hunger that will settle like a wave, like a terrific squall over the upturned faces of the young men on Christopher Street.

The policeman on the beat calls the men by their first name. He calls them Archibald and Turnpike . . . but the distance between the men and him cannot be bridged so easily. They refuse to acknowledge his authority, which is enough to keep them apart. The policeman's wife confuses all messages with lust. All that is not lust is absent. Their son is a mailman. One day he hopes to deliver the mail to the White House and screw the President's wife.

When the people are absent in the early morning hours, each sound is accentuated, exaggerated . . . each sound is being rehearsed for a later occasion . . . People absent themselves behind closed doors after hearing or reading the message: Is there any other way to live? They cloister themselves in small rooms with lousy smells and nervously munch biscuits.

Everything that happens a second time is unbearably familiar, except for the trip through the tunnel. People still tolerate the trip because it breaks the monotony of the sunshine. They remain inside their cars and think.

When my parents went dancing, said the policeman's son to Harry, I was absent. I yelled to them not to leave me, but they didn't hear me, or worse yet, they pretended not to hear me. Now I must have the President's wife.

To Abstain from Sending the Message

Harry has finally destroyed his play. It ran to eight hours with only two brief intermissions. All of the main characters, who resemble Harry in appearance, died either from suffocation, strangulation, or knife wounds. Harry had spent five long years working on the drama . . . he worried and brooded a lot. There was a certain satisfaction in destroying the play, the satisfaction people take when they cut off a finger. Good riddance . . . now I'll have fewer hangnails. It is the second drama Harry has destroyed. How many dramas does a man have in him?

The next day Harry started on a new play. It was about a man who jumped into the river to save another man from drowning. The man who jumped in resembled Harry, so did the man who was drowning. Neither knew how to swim. When both were fished out of the river, Harry's protagonist jumped in again. The first time, Harry reasons, he intended to save the drowning man. But the second time?

The play can be said to be about Harry and the Hudson River. Of course, to some extent it also included the barges that are towed up and down the river. It was unavoidable that Harry would include the barges. He had such a warm feeling toward them. He started the play with one objective in mind: that it be a happy play. He avoided using the word "abstain." There's no profit to be found in its use. It is droll, said Gwen, that Harry's play revolves around the river. The characters in the play fall into stereotypes: the dramatic Harry, the serious Harry, the miserly Harry, the hunchbacked Harry, the other Harry who is a buffoon, and the melancholy tugboat captain. Everyone who read the play was touched in some manner or form by its bathos. They could not help but pity Harry, and permitted him, this once . . . just one time, so that he would know what ecstasy was like . . . But Harry kept on being troubled by the inequities that made some people happier than others.

One day he met two friends from Minneapolis who were visiting the city. They urged him to accompany them to a whorehouse. At first he was reluctant to go, because it seemed such a tourist thing to do. But finally he agreed. He envisioned fantastic draperies and a marble staircase, and tall women with poodles on the leash. But there were no fancy draperies, no marble staircase, and no poodles. Filled with regret he and his two friends wandered over to a tattoo parlor. Now, at last, the mysterious woman of his dreams would be close to his heart, thought Harry.

The Message Comes Apart

What about those notches that men make on their combs now that guns have been outlawed? The habitual desire to possess another man's wife is regretfully abandoned, but not the need to add the number of hours spent waiting for her in a hotel. The mileage brings us closer, says the mechanic at Gulf. So people dutifully add the mileage. How many miles have you come together? asks the Shell service attendant. We have come apart, softly replies Gwen.

People urgently whisper their name to strangers, and ask themselves: Will we do it again? Somehow the furtive element cannot be removed from the exegesis of love. The furtive lover is sustained by the number of self-inflicted scratches on his face. Harry agrees with Tobias that Gwen is a cut above the ordinary . . .

While browsing in a bookstore, Harry noticed two heavy-set men with beards whispering behind the counter. Two years later he spotted them in a grocery store on 89th Street. This time they were clean shaven. They were buying fruit. They were appraising each apple as if it were a freshly mined diamond. Harry looked at them closely but could not tell them apart. A year later, while traveling through the Florida swamps, he came across them again. They had pitched their tent in a small clearing. They also had a fire going. One of the men was kneeling beside his companion who lay stretched out on the ground. Harry did not know that the prostrate man was dead until he was quite close to the tent. Who are you? he finally managed to ask the kneeling man. The memory of that moment is forever stamped on his mind. Now, I am the survivor, whispered the man.

An Auspicious Message

The universal reaction to the auspicious is to render it useless. The first ten minutes of a film may be considered auspicious if a fist is clenched. As the narration unfolds, a horse is casually put out of its misery. It slumps to the ground, pinning the rider against a bed of roses. The audience remain rooted to their seats. Here and there a few hesitantly push their clenched fists into the air. At times the sky turns a bright orange. An auspicious sign for someone setting off for an unknown destination. A year later the explorer returns, and there is one less unknown place to visit.

In small lofts located in cast-iron buildings metal rods are being manufactured that will play a significant role when the auspicious moment arrives, although no one can tell what form that moment will take. The two musically gifted lovers do not wait for the auspicious moment as they set out to visit an aging aunt. They are all smiles as they ride to the station. The young man is the first to dismount. It is one of those incendiary moments when all of life is on the brink of a new discovery. The zip on his pants has burst open, and despite all desperate and feverish attempts refuses to close again. She felt a sudden relief as he, this pink-cheeked lover of hers, rather than face her in this crisis, stepped in the path of the oncoming train. The auspicious exaggerates . . . it adds another dimension to one's measured reliance upon messages.

KAYANERENHKOWA

A Passage from *Homage to the American Indians*

ERNESTO CARDENAL

Translated by Carlos and Monique Altschul

Sept. Oct.
during these months the migrations take place.
Tanagers from Ohio
        forktail ducks from Oklahoma and Texas
come to Nicaragua.
The cormorant comes from Michigan
                         to Solentiname
        here they call it *pato e chanco*.

        Yes, like airplanes
The New York plane over these lonely places.
          Watching perhaps a color movie
THE PERFECT FURLOUGH starring Tony Curtis
                   and Janet Leigh
                   over Solentiname.
And Canadian ducks
           go
in V formation
         Do they come from Lake Ontario?

During these months
            the sky of Nicaragua is full of migrant birds.
And the plover of the Polar Circle
in the wild cove, this "jungle"*
                        fancy that!
it just flew over Central Park.
                        Or over the United Nations?
Degandawida took his canoe through the lakes . . .

From Niagara Falls to Illinois
            the *Pax Iroquoia*
"We shall all eat the same beaver from the same plate"
Not only absence of war.
                        The Iroquois peace
was no cold war. They had
the same word for "Peace" and for "Law"
Peace was the right behavior.
Justice in behavior.
The practice of justice among individuals and nations.
Good government was Peace.
            "This it is to be strong, O Chiefs:
            never to be in wrath, not to have quarrels"
Kayanerenhkowa ("the Great Peace")
            Tarachiwagon, the Great Spirit, inspired it.
The League of Nations was called the "Great Peace"
                        and it was sacred.
The priests, the chiefs of the League.
The ax buried so deep so deep
"that nobody should ever see it again in the future"
            But the French gave cannons to the Susquehannock
It was the fur trade . . .

Degandawida the Huron
            who created the New Mentality
(his name means "Master of the Things")
had visions of a new policy.

* In English in the original Spanish text.

Hiawatha the Onondaga
                    "the one who combs"
(because he combed the snakes out of the minds of men)
was the poet.
He invented the wampum—writing with shells—
and built beautiful stories with shells.
Degandawida took his canoe through the lakes
looking for the smoke on the shore
                                    the smoke
of councils.
                    Rowing always toward the Dawn.
He crossed Lake Ontario (*Sqanyadaii-yo,* "the Great Beautiful
                                                    Lake")
            and no smoke rose.
The Iroquois were at war.
                            The villages
were silent
            surrounded by stockades.
Kayanerenhkowa!!! he shouted

He carried the Mentality of the Master of Life.
            The Good News of Peace
to the camps. Tell the chiefs:
There will be no more wars in the towns
                            the villages will have peace

People should love one another, he said.
A message in the shape of the Meeting House
where there are many fires
                            one for each family
and all together are like one large family
also thus: a union of nations
each nation with the bonfire of its council
and all together will be
                    a great Kanonsionni (Meeting House)

And instead of killing, they will think
                            Degandawida said.
He arrived at the nation of the Pedernal (the Mohawks)
and one afternoon he camped by the Mohawk River
                            (New York)

he sat under a tree and smoked his pipe.
      There the League of Nations was founded
      by the Mohawk River (New York)
One afternoon by the lake
Hiawatha the poet was sad
He picked shells on the bank
      and strung them in 3 lines to symbolize his sadness.
And when he lighted his fire, he said:
      "When someone is sad
      as I am now
      I will comfort him with these strings of shells . . ."
(Degandawida came near Hiawatha's smoke)
      ". . . the strings of shells will be words
      and these words that are in my hands
      will be true"
He came near and picked Hiawatha's shells
         and put them together with others
      and thus
the 2 of them made
      the laws of the Great Peace
the New Laws with shells
each law expressed by a line of shells
      the Words of the Great Peace
for the Oneida the Onondaga the Cayuga the Seneca
   the shells of the lake made song
      as the lake sings in the night with its shells
and that song is still sung
in the reservation at night
by the fire.
That was long ago, the Iroquois say
the creation of that UN
      "in the darkness of the past and the abyss of time"
        (1450?)

And the cormorant comes from Michigan . . .
The sun is setting. The jet over La Venada.
Its wake has stayed
      in the sky, long
        looooooooong chalk line
like the Island of La Venada.

The air-colored lake
and Cosme's motorboat like floating in the air.
"Look at it sparkle . . ." Don Rafael tells me. Don Rafael.
Look at it . . .
                              Mirror of the Great Spirit!
There they go, there they go, flying in V
                              black V V V V V V V
the Canadian ducks
                              like flying squadrons
but they change leaders
                              and the planes do not change formation.
They probably come from Lake Ontario. They will return
                              to Lake Ontario, a new duck
each time at the tip of the V, but always
northward like the needle of a compass
                              carrying spring!

Degandawida said
in his first speech of those United Nations:
"The Fire of the Council of the Confederacy of Nations . . . !
But the bonfires of the nations will burn on
and that of each clan
and that of each family
and the bonfire of women and of men
AND THEY WILL NOT BE EXTINGUISHED . . . !"
          And the League of Nations was founded with songs
          delegations in a circle around the fire
                    Mohawks and Senecas East of the fire
                    Oneidas and Cayugas West of the fire
                    Onondagas North of the fire
all singing the same song as a choir.

And at the close of the First Session of the United Nations:
                    "My work is done. I
                    will enter into the earth. There
                    I shall hear how men behave
                    in the Meeting House I gave them.
                    If the Great Peace ever fails
                    if it ever fails
                    utter my name in the thicket.
                    In the loneliness. And I will return."

They buried axes arrows
        "We have cleaned the earth
            from these things produced by an Evil Mind"
And later the dream of a greater adventure
the meeting around a fire
of *all* the nations of the earth
          the nations of "all the woods on earth"

              A beaver on the plate. Without a knife
            so that nobody should get hurt
             so that no blood is shed

Later, for many years, the hope
that the French would join the League.
        "If you love our souls as you say
        love also our bodies.
        Let us be one nation."
To show their good will
they would deliver themselves unarmed to the French.
With women and children and old men. NOT
as hostages. But
        "to make one nation of the entire earth"
And the march to Quebec—loaded with shells—
but on their way they were attacked by the Algonquins.
The French traded with the Hurons . . .
The talks with the Hurons were blocked.
The agreements with the Hurons, always canceled.
Economic reasons . . . The so-called fur trade . . .
For the Iroquois said: "one nation"
"let us make one people and one nation"
and the French traded with the Hurons.
And the French gave cannon to the Susquehannock.
        "Let us tame the torrents of the river"
And they sent 3 canoes of peace to the French.
Those canoes waiting by the fortress.
          "The land will be beautiful, they screamed
          the river will not have waves
          we will live everywhere without fear"
and that evening around the fire with the French
around the symbolic fire:

"Our faces will melt with yours
so that we shall also have beards
and will all become one face"
And the Nation of the Thirteen Fires?
The Nation of the Thirteen Fires did not
                    enter the League either.

O
    there went the *ah-weh-ah-ah*.
            It rowed with folded wings.
When the Indians left the Great Lakes
it opened its wings and flew away
and did not come back.

The sound of a radio comes with the wind, from Saba's island.
Saba's radio. Saba (the *cariba*, Don Rafael calls her).
Cormorants in line with unfolded wings
            like old shirts on a clothesline.
They wet their tails before flying.
                    Here and in Lake Michigan.
                    Among the buoys of Lake Michigan.
The lakes had a soul, for the Onondaga.
The laws, *talked* in wampum
                    And the treaties in wampum.
            They never broke a wampum
although in treaty after treaty they lost all their land.
The sun sets. Calm lake. In its heart. And an Onondaga moon.
Flying at water level.
                    Tanagers from Ohio. From Kentucky.
                    Like Merton's letter last Tuesday.
And Kennedy Airport so close to Solentiname.
            A radio on an island of a Caribbean Indian.
(Saba brought me oranges)

                    We shall all eat the same beaver
                        from the same plate.
Suddenly a fire in the forest, forms spinning
between the fire and the shade, and their shadows spinning
tan-tan   tan-tan   tan-tan, red tattoos

redder now that the flames rise, ah uuuuuuuum
  also children and dogs prancing
     girls with shells, with
 wampum. Ah uuuuuuuuum. The fire dies off.
They left. And they disappeared from history.
But after the traffic and the neon lights of Syracuse
and beyond the highways in the suburbs, motels
filling stations, and still more neon lights, HAM & EGGS
          at night
behind the large factories, you get to the reservations
a little valley, where that Iroquois said
      by the old Ford that does not work
  "we will rise again
  and the world will listen to us"

The Good News of Peace for the camps
The Good News of Peace (not AP)
The dead on Roosevelt Avenue. AP was there
    and did not tell.
A man jumped into the middle of the street with arms
         outspread
    ENOUGH!!!
  and they riddled him with bullets.
Another Somoza will be president.
You told us to call you in the loneliness.
And I am here in Solentiname!
Degandawida! Degandawida!
The murmur as of an outboard motor coming this way
Yet no motor comes this way:
   the airplane
   of the Nation of the 13 Fires . . .
The flight to Panama.
   The friends are not many, and they are far.
News from everywhere is bad.
    If you are as sad as I am now
    I will comfort you with my wampum,
       or with my old Underwood.

With shells. With these typewriter keys.
      Not the teletypes.
   And these words in my hands will be true.

It is the time of the wading birds in Solentiname.
And that of the sad bird that sings *Fucked up*
The last cormorant is gone.
Are the lights on
              at the UN?
DEGANDAWIDA! DEGANDAWIDA!

And where are the jets going?
Are they going
toward Vietnam?

COGWHEELS

RYUNOSUKE AKUTAGAWA

Translated by Cid Corman and Susumu Kamaike

TRANSLATORS' NOTE: *Ryunosuke Akutagawa was born in Tokyo in 1892. A brilliant student of literature, he studied under Soseki Natsume, the famed Japanese writer (sensei) who died of ulcer trouble at the age of fifty in 1916. In order to devote himself to writing, Akutagawa taught English until shortly after his marriage in 1918. He subsequently visited both China and Russia, and had three sons (born in 1920, 1922, and 1925). He committed suicide by an overdose of sleeping pills on July 24, 1927—the same year in which* Cogwheels *was written. The many literary allusions throughout the only too convincingly autobiographical narrative find sufficient meaning within the context; most of them are to classical Chinese materials.*

1   RAINCOAT

From a summer resort some distance away, taking my bag along, I picked up a car to a station on the Tokaido Line,[1] going to attend a wedding reception for an acquaintance of mine. On either side of the road the car traveled there were only largely pine trees. It was rather doubtful about making the Tokyo-bound train in time. In the car with me was a barber. He was as plump as a peach and

29

with a short beard. With my mind on the time I spoke with him intermittently.

"Strange. I hear So and So's house is haunted even by day."

"*Even* by day."

Looking out at the far hills of pine bathed in the afternoon sun, I satisfied him with occasional responses.

"Not in good weather, though. I hear it appears mostly on rainy days."

"I'm surprised it bothers to appear just to get wet on rainy days."

"No joke, I assure you! . . . And they say the ghost does its haunting in a raincoat."

With a honk of its horn the car pulled up by the station. I took leave of the barber and went into the station. Just as I'd imagined, the train had left only minutes before. On a bench in the waiting room one man in a raincoat stared vacantly out. I remembered the tale just heard. But let it go with a faint smile and decided to go to a café in front of the station anyhow to wait for the next train.

It was a café that scarcely merited the name. I sat at a table in a corner and ordered a cup of cocoa. The oilcloth covering the table had a large crosswork of thin blue lines on a white ground. But each edge of it already showed filthy canvas. I sipped the cocoa, which smelled like animal glue, and looked around the empty café. On the dirty wall were pasted many strips of paper with the menu: "a bowl of rice with egg-and-chicken topping," "beef cutlet," etc.

"Fresh eggs. Cutlet."

The strips of paper made me realize I was out in the country around the Tokaido Line. Here electric locomotives ran through cabbage and wheat fields. . . .

It was close to sunset by the time I boarded the next train. I usually went second class, but decided it would be simpler third class.

The train was rather crowded. In front of me and behind me were primary school girls coming back from Oiso or somewhere else on an excursion. While I lit a cigarette I looked the group of students over. They were all in good spirits. And they were generally chattering away.

"Hey, Mr. Cameraman, what's a love scene like?"

"Mr. Cameraman," in front of me, who seemed to be with the excursion, managed to evade the issue. But one girl of about fourteen or fifteen kept firing questions at him. And noticing she had an an infected nose I couldn't help smiling. Then there was a girl of twelve or thirteen sitting on the lap of a young woman teacher, holding her neck with one hand and caressing her cheek with the other. Chatting with someone she turned to the teacher to say, "You're pretty, teacher. You have pretty eyes, you know."

They struck me more as grown-up women than as children. Apart, that is, from their nibbling at the rinds of apples and unwrapping caramel after caramel. . . But one who looked like a senior must have inadvertently stepped on someone's foot in passing, near me, and said, "I'm extremely sorry." She alone, more precocious than the others, seemed more like a youngster. With the cigarette in my mouth, I couldn't help ridiculing myself for finding any contradiction in this.

The train, with all its lights on, finally arrived at a station in a certain suburb without my being aware of it. I got off and stood on the platform with a cold wind blowing, then crossed an overpass and decided to wait for the local. Then I saw Mr. T., a company man. We discussed the depression, etc., while waiting. Mr. T was naturally more familiar with this sort of problem than I was. But he sported a turquoise ring that had nothing to do with any depression.

"You have a treasure there, I see."

"This? I had to buy it from a friend who'd been in Harbin on business. He's having a hard go of it now. He split with the co-operative."

Fortunately our train was not very crowded. We sat beside each other and talked about various things. Mr. T. had just come back from his company's Paris office this spring. So there was a tendency to speak of Paris. Stories about Mme. Caillaux, crab dishes, a certain prince touring abroad. . .

"It isn't as bad in France as we think. The French are by nature not given to paying their taxes and it often leads to Cabinet dismissals. . ."

"But the franc's in a slump."

"So the papers say. But once you're in France, you find Japan regarded as a country of floods and earthquakes, other sources of trouble."

At just this moment a man in a raincoat took a seat opposite us. I began to feel somewhat weird and was about to tell Mr. T. of the ghost story I had heard earlier. But turning the handle of his cane to the left, keeping his head straight, he whispered.

"You see the woman over there? In the gray shawl. . ."

"The one with the Western hairdo?"

"Yes, the one with the *furoshiki*[2] under her arm. She was in Karuizawa this summer. Quite dolled up in fancy Western style."

She certainly looked shabby now to anyone. I glanced at her while talking with Mr. T. There was something insane in her frowning face. And she had a sponge that looked like a leopard peeking out of her *furoshiki*.

"At Karuizawa she was having a great time dancing with a young American. What you might call modern. . ."

By the time T. and I parted, the man in the raincoat had vanished without my being aware of it. From the train station, bag still with me, I walked over to a hotel. There were mostly huge buildings on both sides of the street. While walking I suddenly thought of pine woods. And then too there was something strange in my line of vision. Strange? There were incessantly revolving half-transparent cogwheels. I'd had such experiences before.The wheels increased until they blocked all other vision, but it was only a moment or so, and then they gave way and a headache commenced—it was always the same. The eye doctor, noting the blinding vision, had often told me to go easy on the smoking. But the wheels had begun occurring to me before I was twenty, before I'd taken to smoking. Sensing it was beginning again I tested my left eye by covering my right. The left eye, as anticipated, was all right. But behind the right eye when closed countless wheels continued revolving. The buildings to the right gradually out of sight, I walked with difficulty.

By the time I reached the hotel entrance the cogs had gone. But not the headache. I checked my overcoat and hat and reserved a room. Then I rang up a certain magazine publisher and discussed money matters.

The wedding reception dinner seemed to have started already. I sat at the end of a table and dug in with knife and fork. The bride and bridegroom and some fifty or more others at the U-shaped main table all seemed cheerful. But I began feeling more and more depressed under the bright lights. Trying to cut the feeling I chatted with the guest next to me. He was an old man with white whiskers like a lion's. In addition, he was a well-known scholar of the Chinese classics, whose name was familiar to me. So our conversation unconsciously drifted to the classics.

"The *kylin* are, in short, sort of unicorns? And *ho* the phoenix. . ."

Chattering on mechanically I gradually felt the desire to be destructive and not only pretended that Yao and Shun were fictitious figures, but claimed that the author of the *Chronicles of Lu* was of the Han Dynasty. At this point the scholar of Chinese classics could not contain his unhappiness and, turning away from me altogether, cut off my storytelling with a grumble vaguely like that of a tiger.

"If Yao and Shun didn't live, it would mean Confucius was a liar. Saints cannot be liars."

With that the small talk ended. Once more I was back dabbling with knife and fork at the meat before me. There I discovered a tiny creature wriggling at an edge of the meat. It brought to mind the English word *worm*. Surely, like the *kylin* and *ho*, this too was indicative of a legendary beast. I set down knife and fork and gazed instead at the champagne poured into my goblet.

After dinner was finally over, quite ready to lock myself up in the room reserved for me, I walked along the empty corridors. They made me feel more like I was in a prison than in a hotel. But fortunately, at the same time, without my being aware of it the headache had largely subsided.

In addition to the bag, my hat and overcoat had been deposited in the room. My overcoat hanging on the wall looked too much like my upright self, and I at once tossed it into the wardrobe in the corner. Then, over at the dressing table I looked at my face in the mirror determinedly. It revealed the bone beneath the skin. The worm had reappeared again.

Opened the door and went back out into the corridor and walked uncertain of where to turn. Then, in one corner on the way to the lobby a tall lamp with a green shade cast a sharp reflection over a glazed door. Somehow or other this calmed my mind. I sat myself down on a chair before it and started brooding about various things. But five minutes was just about it. Then I noticed on the back of the sofa beside me, again hanging loosely, a raincoat.

"And this is the coldest season now too."

My mind wandering in such a vein I went back down the corridor. In the waiters' room there was no waiter in sight. But some of their conversation fell into my ears in passing. It was in English: "All right," in answer to something. "All right?" I tried to figure out what it was all about. "All right?" "All right?" What on earth was all right?

Of course, my room was quiet. But just to open the door and go in, oddly enough, seemed weird to me. After some hesitancy I finally ventured in. Then, careful not to look into the mirror, I sat on a chair at the desk. The chair was an armchair of lizardlike blue morocco. I opened my bag, pulled out a writing pad, and tried to resume a certain short story. But the pen and ink hung eternal fire. And when finally they moved, or I thought they moved, only the same words appeared, All right. . . All right. . . All right, sir. . . . All right. . .

Ringing by the bed suddenly there was the telephone. Startled I rose and lifting the receiver to my ear answered.

"Who is it?"

"It's me. Me. . ."

On the other end was my older sister's daughter.

"What? What's the matter?"

"Yes. Well, something terrible has happened. So . . . because something terrible's happened, I just called Auntie too."

"Something terrible?"

"Yes. So, please come quick. Quick."

And the telephone on the other end clicked off. I put the receiver back and mechanically pushed the call button. But I was perfectly aware of my hand trembling. The boy was slow in coming. Feeling more pain than impatience, I pushed the button again and again, sensing the meaning of the words "all right," which fate had been trying to get through to me.

My older sister's husband had been run over and killed that afternoon in the country not too far from Tokyo. Furthermore, unrelated to the weather completely, he had been wearing a raincoat. I'm still writing the same short story in this hotel room. There's no one out there going by in the corridor. But from beyond the door there is sometimes heard the flapping of wings. Someone may be keeping a bird.

2 VENGEANCE

I woke about half past eight in this hotel room. But, on getting out of bed, I discovered, oddly enough, that one of my slippers was gone. It was just the sort of thing that would rouse me to fear, anxiety, etc., this past year or two. And it reminded me also of some prince in Greek myth wearing another's sandal. Pushing the bell, I rang for the boy and had him look for the lost slipper. He searched the room with a *quizzical* expression on his face.

"I've found it, here. Here in the bathroom."

"How'd it get there?"

"Maybe a mouse."

After the boy left I had a cup of coffee, without milk, and set about finishing my story. A square window frame of tufa looked out upon a garden of snow. Whenever I stopped writing I would absent-mindedly gaze at the snow. Under the fragrant bush of budding daphne the snow was dirtied by the smoke and soot of the city. The sight of it pained me. I smoked a cigarette, thought of a host of things, and pen was not put to paper. Thought of my wife, my children, most of all, my older sister's husband. . .

He was under suspicion, before committing suicide, of arson. Actually it was inevitable. Before his house was burned down it had been insured for twice its value. Even so, while guilty of perjury, he had been on probation. It was not his suicide, however, that made me uneasy, but that I could never return to Tokyo without seeing a fire. Once there was the fire I saw in the hills from the train, and another time from a car (I was with my wife and children) near Tokiwabashi. Naturally I had a premonition of a fire before his house was, in fact, burned down.

"A fire may break out in our house this year."

"Don't talk like that . . . if there were ever a fire, it would bring a load of problems with it. There isn't enough insurance and . . ."

So we spoke. But there hasn't been any fire and—trying to shake the idea—I picked up my pen again. Not even a single line would come. Finally abandoning my post at the desk I lay down on the bed and began reading Tolstoy's *Polikoushka*. The hero of this novel is a complex personality of vanity, morbidity, and ambition all mixed up. And with a few minor changes, the tragicomedy of his life could pass as a caricature of my own. Particularly did I feel the derisiveness of fate in the tragicomedy of it, and that gradually made me feel weird. After no more than an hour of it I jumped out of bed and threw the book at the window drapery in the corner of the room.

"Damn you!"

And a big mouse appeared scuttling diagonally from under the curtain toward the bathroom. In a bound I was at the bathroom and opened the door, looking for it. Behind the white tub not a sign of it. I felt weird suddenly, and changing into slippers quickly, I went out into the corridor, but not a living thing was in sight.

The corridor, as usual, was as gloomy as a prison. With my head down, going up and down stairs, quite unawares, I found myself suddenly in the kitchen. The room was brighter than might have been expected. And over on one side flames rose abundantly from the range. In passing through I could feel the cold eyes of the cooks in their white hats staring at me. At once I felt myself cast into hell. "God, punish me. Please, don't be offended. I'm going to be ruined." Naturally at that moment such a prayer was bound to come from my lips.

I left the hotel and walked with difficulty the slushy way to my older sister's. The trees in the park along the way had all had their leaves and branches blackened. And each of them had, just like us, a front and back side. It was less displeasing to me than it was intimidating. I remembered the soul that had turned into a tree in Dante's *Inferno* and decided to walk on the street across from the streetcar tracks, where buildings formed a sturdy row. But even there one block was too much.

"Excuse me for stopping you."

It was a fellow of about twenty-two or twenty-three in a uniform with gold buttons. I stared at him wordlessly and noted a mole on the left side of his nose. He, with cap off, addressed me warily.

"Aren't you Mr. A.?"

"Yes,"

"I thought you were . . ."

"What do you want?"

"Nothing. I just wanted to say hello. I'm an admirer of yours, *sensei*. . ."

With that I tipped my hat to him and began to make space between us as rapidly as possible. *Sensei*. *A-sensei*—the title had recently begun to be most distasteful to me. I had come to feel I had committed every imaginable crime. Regardless, I was to be called *sensei* now; whenever possible. I couldn't help feeling something shameful in it. Something? But my materialism shouldn't balk at mysticism. A few months earlier I had written in a little magazine, "I not only have no artistic conscience, but no conscience at all. All I have is nerve. . ."

My older sister had found refuge in a barracks up an alley with her children. Inside the barracks with its brown wallpaper, it looked bleaker than it did outside. Warming our hands over a *hibachi*[3] we spoke of various things. My sister's husband, a man of stocky build, had had no use for me, instinctively, from the start. And he had openly referred to the immorality of my work. I'd never had any friendly conversation with him, due to his looking askance at someone with such ideas. Talking with my sister, I realized that he too had gradually been shot to hell. I heard he actually saw a ghost in a sleeping compartment. But, lighting up a cigarette, I carefully kept talk on the subject simply of money.

"Anyhow, the way it is, I'm just figuring to sell as much as I can."

"I've been figuring the same too. The typewriter should bring in some cash."

"And we have some paintings."

"How about selling N-san's [my sister's husband] portrait? But that's . . ."

I looked up at the unframed Conté crayon portrait on the wall and felt I shouldn't joke so thoughtlessly. I'd heard that his face had been crushed by the train to a tatter of flesh, only his mustache had been left. The story had, in fact, shaken me. His portrait was drawn perfectly in every detail, but his mustache looked somehow unclear. I thought it might be because of the lighting and studied the picture from different angles.

"What're you doing?"

"Nothing . . . just around the mouth of that picture . . ." She turned to look too, for a moment, but said she couldn't see anything off.

"Only the mustache, oddly enough, looks thin, doesn't it?"

What I was seeing was no illusion. But if it wasn't . . . I decided it wiser to leave my sister's before she began fussing about lunch.

"Why don't you stay a bit longer?"

"Tomorrow maybe. . . Today I have to go to Aoyama."

"Oh, there? Something still wrong with your body?"

"I'm taking sleeping drugs as usual. I've got so many. Veronal, Muronal, Trional, Numal . . ."

About thirty minutes later, I entered a building, got on an elevator, and went up to the third floor. There, I tried pushing open the glass door to a restaurant. It wouldn't budge. On it hung a sign inscribed: STORE HOLIDAY. I was more than a little peeved, but after a glance at the apples and bananas displayed on a table the other side of the door, decided to go back on the street again. Two men, who seemed to be office-hands, brushed by me at the entrance, lost in conversation. At just that moment one of them, or so it seemed to me, said: "It's tantalizing."

I stood on the street, waiting for a taxi to come by. It took some time. Usually, though, there never failed to be a yellow cab around. (These yellow cabs for some reason always involved me in accidents.) After a while, however, a lucky green cab was found, and I decided anyway to go to the mental hospital near the Aoyama Cemetery.

"Tantalizing—tantalizing—Tantalus—inferno . . ."

Tantalus myself, in fact—gazing at fruit through the glass door. Cursing the Dante's *Inferno* in my mind's eye, I stared at the driver's back. And the feeling came over me that everything is a lie. Politics, business, art, science—all, in the face of what I now was nothing but so much camouflage of this horrible existence. I was beginning to feel stifled and opened a window. But the feeling wouldn't go away.

The green cab reached Jingu-mae eventually. There was an alleyway leading to the mental hospital. This day, though, of all days, somehow, I couldn't locate it. After getting the cab to scout around for it and then back along the streetcar tracks, I gave it up and decided to get out.

I found the way finally and found myself twisting right and left on a road full of mud puddles. Then, unwittingly, I must have taken a wrong turn, for there I was at the Aoyama Funeral Parlor. It was a building whose gate I hadn't passed since Natsume-sensei's funeral, about ten years before. Ten years ago I wasn't very happy. But at least I was peaceful. I noticed the gravelwork beyond the gate and reminded of the *basho*[4] tree at the Soseki Retreat, I couldn't help feeling that my life had ended. And I also couldn't help feeling that something had drawn me back to this place after ten year's absence.

After leaving the gate of the mental hospital, I took a taxi again and decided to go back to the hotel I'd been at before. But, on leaving the taxi at the hotel entrance, I found a man in a raincoat arguing for some reason with a waiter. With a waiter? No. Not a waiter, but a man in a green uniform in charge of the taxis. The idea of entering the hotel seemed ominous to me and I quickly turned away.

When I reached the Ginza, it was almost sundown. The shops jammed on both sides of the street, the bewildering throngs of people, all combined to depress me more. It disturbed me most that everyone on the street walked nonchalantly, indifferently, as if they were unaware of sin. I kept walking north amid the confusion of twilight and electric lights. Then my eye was caught by a bookstore with magazines and books all piled up. I went in and absent-mindedly browsed some shelves. There was a book titled *Greek Myth* I decided to look at. *Greek Myth*, with a yellow cover, seemed written for children. But one line I read by accident suddenly shook me.

"Even mightiest Zeus cannot vanquish the God of Vengeance...."

I left the shop and went into the crowd. I could feel the God of Vengeance hovering at my back and began wandering witlessly.

3   NIGHT

On one of the shelves upstairs at Maruzen[5] I found Strindberg's *Tale* and read a few pages while standing there. It describes experiences not unlike my own. And it had a yellow cover. I put it back and pulled out a thick book my hand happened to fall on. In it what should there be but an illustration of cogs with eyes and noses not unlike human beings! It was a collection of pictures by inmates of a lunatic asylum assembled by some German. Even in my depression, my spirit could be felt rising in rebellion and with the desperation of an addicted gambler kept opening book after book. Oddly enough, almost every book had clearly hidden stings in its sentences and illustrations. Every book? Even in *Madame Bovary*, which I had read many times before, I felt I was only the bourgeois Monsieur Bovary in the end.

Upstairs at Maruzen, almost nightfall, there seemed no other customer beside myself. I browsed around the bookshelves in the electric light. I stopped at a shelf with the title *Religion* on it and removed a book with a green cover. One chapter in the table of contents read: "Four Deadly Foes—Suspicion, Fear, Vanity, and Sensuality." With the words, at once, my spirit again rose rebellious. Those foes were only other names for Sensitivity and Intelligence. It was unbearable to feel the traditional as depressing as the modern. The book in my hand brought to mind the pen name I'd once used, Juryo Yoshi. It was the name of the young man in Chuang-tse who had forgotten the boy from Juryo who had attempted to ape the stride of one from Kantan and could only end up crawling home. I must be Juryo Yoshi now to everybody. And I,

when I hadn't yet been consigned to hell, had used the name—
I, with a shelfload of books behind me, tried to banish the conceit
and went into a poster showroom just off to one side. There, in one
of the posters, a knight who seemed to be St. George was stabbing
a winged dragon to death. On top of this, the half-revealed frown-
ing face of the knight under the helmet resembled one of my
enemies. I also recalled Toryu's art in the *Kanbishi* and, without
passing through the showroom, went down the broad staircase.

Walking along Nihonbashi now, in the dark, I kept thinking of
the word *toryu*. It was the name of my inkstick too, I'm sure. The
man who had given it to me was a certain entrepreneur. He failed
in a variety of businesses and finally went to wrack and ruin. I
found myself looking up into the sky and thinking how small the
earth is amongst all the stars—and so how much smaller I was. But
the sky, which had been clear all day, had become cloudy without
my realizing it. At once I felt that things had taken a hostile turn
toward me and decided to take asylum in a café.

"Asylum" was precisely what it was. I somehow felt something
soothing in the rosy tint of the wall and relaxed at a table. Fortu-
nately there were only a few other clients there. I sipped a cup of
cocoa and started to pull on a cigarette, as usual. The smoke rose
in a faint blue stream up the rosy wall. The harmonious mingling
of the soft colors was agreeable to me. But after a time I discovered
a portrait of Napoleon on the wall to my left and began to feel
uneasy again. When Napoleon was only a student, he had written
on the last page of his geography notebook: "Saint Helena, a small
island." It might have been, as we say, only a coincidence. But it
must have made even Napoleon shiver eventually. . .

Gazing at Napoleon, I thought about my own work. And there
burst upon me certain phrases in "A Fool's Words." (Especially
the words, "Life is more hellish than hell itself.") And also the
hero's fate in my "Hell Screen"—a painter called Yoshihide. Then
. . . smoking I looked around the café trying to escape such mem-
ories. I had taken shelter here no more than five minutes earlier.
Already the place had undergone a complete change. What made
me most uncomfortable was the fact that the chairs and tables of
imitation mahogany did not go with the rosy walls. Afraid I should
fall into an agony imperceptible to others, I tried to get out of the
café by quickly tossing down a silver coin.

"Sir, it's twenty sen. . ."

I had tossed down a copper.

Walking alone along the street, feeling humiliated, I suddenly recalled my house in the remote pine wood. It wasn't my foster parents' place off in the suburbs, but a house I rented for my family, in which I was the master. I used to live in such a house also about ten years before. But for one reason or another I'd thoughtlessly taken up again with my folks. At the same time I started to become a slave, a tyrant, an impotent egoist. . .

When I reached the hotel again, it was almost ten. I'd been walking for so long a space that I hadn't the strength to go to my room and sat instead on a chair in front of the fireplace where a huge log was burning. I began to think of the long piece I'd been planning. It was a long piece in which common people from the Suiko to the Meiji Era would be used as heroes, in a sequence of more than thirty chronological short stories. Some sparks leapt up, and I remembered the bronze statue in front of the Imperial Palace. The statue was in armor and helmet, high astride a steed—as if it were Fealty itself. But its enemy was—

"A lie!"

Again I sped from distant past to immediate present. The man who luckily came over then was an older sculptor. He was wearing a velvet coat and pulling on a short goatee. I rose and shook the hand he offered. (This was not a habit of mine. I simply followed his, for he had spent half his life in Paris and Berlin.) Oddly enough, however, his hand was slimy as a reptilian skin.

"Are you staying here?"

"Yes. . ."

"To do your work?"

"Yes, I'm doing my work too."

He looked me straight in the face. I felt the scrutiny of a detective in his eyes.

"Hey, how about coming to my room for some talk?"

I spoke aggressively. (It was one of my bad habits to assume quickly an attitude of challenge, though I had no courage.) He smiled and asked in return, "Where's your room?"

Shoulder to shoulder walking through softly speaking foreigners, as if we were good friends, we returned to my room. In my room he sat with the mirror behind him. And he started talking about a lot of things. A lot of things?—mostly, in fact, stories about women. I was undoubtedly one of those condemned to hell because of the sins I had committed. So the tales of vice made me all the gloomier. For a moment I felt puritanical and began to despise such women.

"Take a look at S-ko-san's lips. Because of her kissing so many men, she . . ."

I shut my mouth suddenly and looked at his back in the glass. He had a yellow plaster pasted on just below his ear.

"Because of her kissing so many men?"

"She seems to be that type."

He smiled and nodded. I felt him always intent upon trying to pry my secret open. But our talk was not off women yet. I felt more embarrassed for my lack of courage than that I hated him, and could only become more depressed.

After he had finally gone, I lay down and began to read *An-ya Koro*.[6] Every spiritual struggle that its hero undergoes was moving to me. I felt how stupid I was, compared with him, and found myself weeping without realizing it. At the same time the tears brought me peace. But not for long. Again my right eye began to sense those half-transparent cogs. The cogs, turning incessantly always, gradually increased in number. Fearful of a headache I left the book beside the pillow, took 0.8 grams of Veronal, and decided to try to get a good night's rest anyhow.

But in my dream I was gazing into a pool. Many boys and girls were swimming there or diving under water. I walked into the pine wood leaving the pool behind. Then someone spoke to me behind me, "Father." I turned round for a moment and found my wife standing by the pool. And felt an intense regret.

"Father, towel?"

"I don't need it. Keep an eye on the children."

I walked on. But where I was walking had become a platform before I knew it. It looked like a country station with a long hedge around the platform. A student from the university, called H., and an old woman were standing there too. They noticed me and came over and addressed me one at a time.

"A big fire, wasn't it?"

"I just managed to escape too."

It seemed to me I had seen the old woman before. And I felt exhilaration in talking to her. Then a train quietly pulled in puffing out smoke. I got on the train alone and walked on in between beds with white cloth hanging down on both sides. I noticed a naked woman very like a cadaver lying on one bed facing me. It must have been that of some madman's daughter—the God of my vengeance. . .

No sooner did I wake than I jumped out of bed, in spite of myself. The electricity kept the room as bright as before. But somewhere there were sounds of wings flapping, mice gnawing. I opened the door, went out into the corridor, and quickly made my way to the fireplace. I sat myself down and started gazing at the feeble glow. A boy in a white uniform came in to replenish the fire.

"What's the time?"

"About 3:30, sir."

Way off in a corner of the lobby a woman, who looked American, was busy reading a book alone. Even from where I was it was clear that she was wearing a green dress. Somehow or other I felt relieved and decided to wait quietly for daybreak. Like an old man calmly awaiting death after the long suffering of an illness. . .

4   STILL?

Finally I finished the short story in the hotel room and decided to send it to a certain magazine. Actually the money to be earned from it was less than that needed to cover the bill at the hotel for a week. But I was content to have done the work and decided to visit a certain bookshop on the Ginza for some spiritual tonic.

On the asphalt pavement in the winter sun were many scraps of wastepaper. They all looked exactly like roses. I felt somehow in good spirits and entered the bookshop. It was rather neater than usual. A young girl in glasses was discussing something with a clerk, and the talk didn't altogether grate on my nerves. However, remembering the wastepaper roses on the street, I decided to buy *The Collected Dialogues of Anatole France* and *The Collected Letters of Prosper Mérimée*.

With the two books under my arm, I went into a café. I decided to wait for a cup of coffee to be brought to a table at the far end of the room. On the other side sat a couple who seemed like mother and son. The son was younger than myself, but an exact copy of me. And they were conversing as if they were lovers, intimately. Watching them I began to sense that the son was aware of providing some sort of sexual satisfaction to his mother as well. It was a kind of relation I knew from experience. Also, it was the sort of instance of willfulness that makes the world a hell. But I was fearful of falling prey to anxieties again and began to read *The Collected Letters of Prosper Mérimée*, taking advantage of the coffee served. The letters revealed in their wit the same aphoristic bite as in the novels. Such sentences gave an iron edge to my feelings. (One of my weak points was in being easily influenced by such twists.) I was soon done with the coffee and, feeling relaxed and carefree, left the café.

Along the street I browsed the shopwindows one by one. A frame shop displayed a portrait of Beethoven. The portrait was the image of genius, hair on end. I couldn't help feeling it ridiculous . . .

Just then I caught sight of an old friend of mine from high-school days. A university professor of applied chemistry now, he held a big bulging bag and one of his eyes was clotted red.

"What's the matter with your eye?"

"This? Just conjunctivitis."

Then I remembered that I had often—fourteen or fifteen years earlier—suffered the same disease out of a feeling of affinity. But I said nothing. He patted me on the shoulder and started talking about our friends. The talk led him to take me to a café.

"It's a long time since we last met. Maybe not since the ceremony for the monument to Shushunsui."[7]

After lighting a cigar he spoke across the marble table.

"Yes. That Shushun. . ."

I don't know why, but I couldn't pronounce the word Shushunsui correctly. Because it was Japanese it made me feel all the more uneasy. But he chatted on about a host of things without noticing. About the novelist K., about a bulldog he had bought, about the poison gas lucite . . .

"You don't seem to be writing much. I did read your *Death Register*, however . . . Is that one autobiographical?"

"Yes, that's autobiographical."

"It's rather morbid. Are you okay these days?"

"I'm forced to take drugs always, as you know."

"I suffer from insomnia these days too."

"What do you mean 'too'?"

"Why I hear you also have insomnia . . . right? It's dangerous, you know . . ."

There was something of a smile revealed in the left eye suffering from conjunctivitis. Before answering I could sense that I was going to have difficulty pronouncing the final syllable of the word *insomnia.*

"It's natural for the son of someone mad."

Less than ten minutes later I was again walking along the street. Scraps of wastepaper on the asphalt did not quite resemble the faces of men. Then a woman with bobbed hair approached from the opposite direction. From a distance she looked beautiful. But when she came near me she revealed not only wrinkles, but ugliness. And she looked pregnant. In spite of myself I turned away from her and turned into a wide sidestreet. But now for some time I had started to feel hemorrhoidal pains. It was pain I could relieve only by a hip-bath.

"A hip bath—Beethoven used to take hip baths too."

Immediately the smell of sulphur used in the baths struck my nostrils. Naturally, there was no sulphur apparent on the street. I remembered the wastepaper roses again and walked on as steadily as possible.

An hour later, confined to my room again, I sat at the desk and started another short story. The pen moved fluently upon the paper to my own surprise. But after a few hours it stopped, as if something invisible to me had intervened. I felt compelled to rise from the desk and walk back and forth around the room. The illusion of expansiveness was most unusual this time. With a sort of savage joy I felt I had neither parents nor wife nor children, that all I had was the life that flowed from my pen.

But after four or five minutes I was called to the telephone. I answered many times, but the telephone merely repeated its ambiguous words. It sounded anyhow like *more.* Finally I abandoned the telephone and started pacing the room again. But the word *more,* strangely enough, weighed upon me.

"More—mole . . ."

Mole is English for *mogura.* The association was not a happy one to me either. And within seconds I was fighting against *mole* as *la mort. La mort*—death in French—made me feel uneasy. As death had pressed upon my sister's husband, so did it seem now to be pressing on me. But even in my uneasiness I felt something funny. And I found myself smiling unwittingly. Why did it strike me funny? I wasn't sure. I stood before the mirror, which I hadn't done for some time, and faced my reflection. Naturally my face was smiling. While staring at it, I remembered the alter ego. My alter ego—the German *Doppelgänger*—had fortunately never much resembled me. But K.'s wife, who had become an American movie star, happened to see my alter ego in the corridor of the Imperial Theater. (I remember my embarrassment at being addressed suddenly by Mrs. K.: "I'm sorry I didn't say hello to you the other day.") Then a former one-legged translator also happened to see my alter ego in a tobacco shop on the Ginza. Death might come to my alter ego rather than to me. Even if it occurred to me—I turned away from the mirror and returned to the desk before the window. A faded lawn and a pool could be seen through the square frame of tufa. Gazing at the garden I remembered some notebooks and unfinished plays I had burned in a distant pine wood. Picking up my pen, I started writing at the new story again.

5　SHAKKO (*RED LIGHT*)[8]

The sunlight began to torment me. Like a mole, I kept the curtains drawn and, with the electricity on, kept plugging away at the story. Then, fagged out, I opened Taine's *History of English Literature* and read about the lives of the poets. They had all been unhappy. Even the giants of the Elizabethan Age—even Ben Jonson, the most distinguished scholar of his day, would find himself so worn with anxiety that he started seeing Roman and Carthaginian armies battling upon his big toe. I couldn't help feeling pleasure, not without a measure of malice, in such misfortunes.

At night with an east wind blowing hard (for me a good omen), I went through the basement out into the street and decided to visit an old man I knew. He worked by himself as a caretaker in the attic of a Bible company and devoted most of his time to prayer and reading. Warming our hands over a *hibachi* we spoke of various things under a cross on the wall. Why did my mother go insane? Why did my father fail in business? Why was I being punished? He was familiar with these arcane issues and with a strange solemn smile would talk with me at length and at ease. And at times in his pithy phrases caught life in all its caricature. I couldn't help admiring the hermit in his attic. But in talking with him, I found him feeling certain affinities—

"The gardener's daughter is lovely, good-natured—and so kind to me."

"How old is she?"

"Eighteen this year."

It might be a sort of fatherliness in him. But it was hard not to sense some passion in his eyes. And the apples he offered me unwittingly on their yellowed rinds revealed unicorns. (I often found mythical creatures in wood grain and in the cracks in coffee cups.) The unicorns were, no doubt, *kylin* (the Chinese unicorns). I recalled that a hostile critic had once called me a "prodigy *(kirinji)* of the 1910s" and suddenly felt that this attic with its cross was no safe place either.

"How have you been lately?"

"Edgy, as usual."

"Drugs won't cure it. Why don't you become a Christian?"

"If even *I* could become . . ."

"There's nothing hard about it. If you just believe in God, in Christ the Son of God, and the miracles Christ did . . ."

"Devils I believe in . . ."

"Then why not believe in God? If you believe shadow, I don't see how you can help believing light also."

"But there's some darkness that has no light in it."

"Darkness without light?"

All I could say was nothing. He was walking in darkness too. But as long as there was darkness, he believed in a light that went with it. This was the only point of logical difference between us. But to me it was an unbridgeable abyss . . .

"But there is light really. We have miracles to prove it . . . Even nowadays miracles occur."

"Miracles are the doings of devils . . ."

"Where do your devils come in?"

I was tempted to tell him of my experiences this past year or two. However, I couldn't help fearing that he would tell my wife and children and that I might be sent back to the asylum as my mother had been.

"What's that over there?"

The plump old man turned around to the ancient bookshelves and made a grimace rather like Pan.

"That's a set of Dostoevski. Have you read *Crime and Punishment?*"

Naturally I'd had a penchant for Dostoevski some ten years earlier and had read four or five books of his. But moved by his saying at random *Crime and Punishment,* I borrowed the book from him and decided to go back to the hotel. The street blazing electric lights and so crammed with people oppressed me. At this point it would have been unbearable to have met anyone I knew. I tried to move through darker sidestreets and progressed like a thief.

After a bit, however, I started to feel my stomach ache. Only a glass of whisky could cure this pain. I found a bar and tried to push my way through the door. At the tight bar the smoke was rising thick, and some young people, who looked like they might be artists, were drinking *sake* together. Amidst it all was also a girl, her hair over her ears, plucking away at a mandolin quite earnestly. At once I felt uncertain and turned back without having gone past the door. I found my shadow swaying to right and to left witlessly. And the light shining upon me, strangely enough, was red. I stopped. But my shadow kept wavering from side to side just as before. I turned around timidly and finally noticed a stained-glass lantern hanging from the eave of the bar. The lantern was moving slowly, moved by a strong wind . . .

The next place I went into was a basement restaurant. I stood at the bar and ordered a whisky.

I poured the whisky into a glass of soda and sipped it silently. Next to me were two men of about thirty or so, who looked like journalists, talking in a low voice. They were speaking in French. I kept my back to them, but felt their eyes upon me. In fact, they impinged upon me like an electric current. They knew my name, definitely, and were gossiping about me.

"Bien . . . très mauvais . . . pourquoi? . . ."

"Pourquoi? . . . le diable est mort! . . ."

"Oui, oui . . . d'enfer . . ."

I tossed a silver coin on the bar (the last real money I had on me) and decided to get out of that basement. On the street with the night breeze blowing my nerve strengthened and my stomach-ache eased off. I remembered Raskolnikov and felt a desire to repent for everything. But, not only to myself, but even to my family, it would surely have been a tragedy. And it was questionable whether the desire was real or not. If only my nerves were as strong as those of ordinary men—but I needed to go somewhere for that to happen. To Madrid, or Rio, or Samarkand . . .

Just then a small white sign at the eave of a shop made me feel uneasy. It bore the trade-mark of wings painted on an automobile tire. It reminded me of Icarus with his artificial wings. His attempt to fly high, his wings singed by the sun's heat, his finally being drowned in the sea. To Madrid, or Rio, or Samarkand—how could I help laughing at such a silly dream? At the same time I couldn't help thinking of Orestes pursued by the gods of vengeance.

I walked on a dark street by a canal. Then I remembered my foster parents' home in the suburbs. Of course, they must be waiting for me to return. Probably my children too—but when I returned— I couldn't help fearing there would be some force there to restrain me, naturally. The lapping water of the canal lifted a junkboat beside me. From the bottom of the boat a faint light shone. There too there must be a family, men and women, living together. Hating each other and still loving each other enough . . . but I roused my mind to continue the struggle and decided to return to the hotel, feeling the whisky in me.

Back at the desk I returned to my reading of Mérimée's *Letters*. It quietly began to revive me. But when I discovered that Mérimée had in his later years become a Protestant, I suddenly sensed he was wearing a mask. He was groping in darkness just as we were. In darkness?—*An-ya Koro* began to assume fearful proportions for me. I turned to Anatole France's *Collected Dialogues* to forget my depression. But this Pan of modern times also bore a cross . . .

About an hour thereafter the boy brought me a batch of letters. One of them was from a bookshop in Leipzig asking me for an essay on "Modern Women in Japan." Why do they look to *me* for such an article? There was a postscript (in English), handwritten: "We would appreciate also along with it a portrait of a woman—but in black-and-white as in Japanese paintings." The words reminded me of the whisky Black & White, and I tore the letter to shreds. I broke the seal of one of the other letters, quite at random, and scanned the yellow letter paper. It was from a youngster, some-one unknown to me. But after a few lines the words "Your *Hell Screen* . . ." irritated me. The third one I opened was from my nephew. After a good deep breath, I plunged into reading about the family problems, etc. But even this letter bowled me over at its close.

"I'm sending you a copy of the second edition of the *Shakko Anthology* . . ."

Shakko! It felt like someone was deriding me and I sought shelter outside the room. In the corridor there was no one. I leaned against the wall with one hand for support and made my way to the lobby. I took a chair and decided to light a cigarette. Somehow it was an Airship cigarette. (I had only smoked Star cigarettes since coming to this hotel.) Artificial wings loomed before my eyes again. I decided to call the boy over and have him get me two packets of Star. But if I could believe the boy, unfortunately all the Stars had been sold out.

"But we have Airships, sir . . ."

I shook my head and looked around the vast lobby. Over on the other side were some foreigners at a table talking. One of them, a woman in a red dress, seemed to be looking at me and speaking to the others in a whisper.

"Mrs. Townshead . . ."

Something beyond my power to see came to me nevertheless through the whispering. The name of Mrs. Townshead was, of course, unfamiliar to me. Even if it were the name of that woman there—I rose and, half crazed with fear, decided to go back to my room.

Back in the room I thought of calling a certain mental hospital. But to go there meant death to me. After much hesitancy I started reading *Crime and Punishment* to distract myself. The page I turned to, however, was from *The Brothers Karamazov*. Assuming I had made a mistake in my acquisition, I looked at the cover. *Crime and Punishment*—the book must be *Crime and Punishment*. In the bookbinder's error, in the fact that I had opened to this page wrongly bound, I felt a fateful finger moving and inevitably read on. But before I had finished even the one page I began to feel my body trembling. It was a passage of Ivan's being tormented by the Devil's Inquisition. Ivan, Strindberg, de Maupassant, myself, in this room . . .

Only sleep could save me in this state. The sleeping drugs were all gone through, before I realized it. I couldn't bear the torment without sleep. With a courage born of desperation I had a cup of coffee brought in and decided to keep writing frantically. Two, five, seven, ten pages—the manuscript was dashed off. I filled the story with supernatural creatures. One of the creatures depicted myself. But exhaustion finally made my head limp. I withdrew from the desk and lay on my back in the bed. I must have slept about forty to fifty minutes. I felt someone whispering in my ear, which awoke and brought me to my feet, the words:

"Le diable est mort."

Outside the tufa window day was about to break shiveringly. I stood at the door and looked around the empty room. In the windowpane I noticed a small scene of the sea beyond a yellowish pine wood. I went to the window with some timidity, to see what had evoked the picture was the withered grass and pool in the garden. But the image had brought to mind a sort of nostalgia for my house.

I decided I would go home after I had called one of the magazine companies and found some source of income, at nine o'clock. Books, papers, gear were stuffed back into my bag on the desk.

6 AIRPLANE

I picked up a car from a station on the Tokaido Line to a summer resort some distance away. For some reason, despite the chilly weather, the driver was wearing a raincoat. Feeling something queer in this coincidence, I tried to keep looking out the window so as not to see him, if possible. Just beyond a place where small pine trees were growing, probably along an old path, I saw a funeral procession passing. There seemed to be no white lanterns or shrine lanterns in the procession. But gold and silver artificial flowers were silently swaying before and after the bier . . .

When I finally got home I had a few very peaceful days, due to my wife and children and opiates. The upstairs commanded a modest view of the sea beyond the pine woods. At the desk upstairs, hearing the pigeons cooing, I decided to work only mornings. In addition to pigeons and crows, sparrows would also alight on the porch. It was a joy to me. "A magpie enters the hall"—with pen in hand, whenever they came, the words came to me too.

One warm cloudy afternoon I went to the grocer's to buy some ink. The only ink they had was sepia. Sepia ink made me more uncomfortable than any other. I had to get out of the shop and strolled along the busy street alone. A near-sighted foreigner of forty or so went strutting by. He was Swedish and suffered from paranoia and lived nearby. And his name was Strindberg. When I passed him, the event physically weighed on me.

The street was only a few blocks long. But in walking the distance a dog, black on one side, passed me four times. Turning the corner, I recalled Black & White whisky. And I remembered too that Strindberg's cravat was black and white. It couldn't be just a coincidence. And if it wasn't—I felt as if only my head had been walking and paused for a moment. Behind a wire fence by the road a faint rainbow-colored glass bowl had been discarded. On its base the bowl had a design like a wing stamped. A number of sparrows flew down from the pine tops. But when they came near it, each, as if in common accord, flew off together into the sky . . .

I went to my wife's parents' house and sat on a rattan chair in the garden. In a wire coop at one corner of the garden many white Leghorns gadded quietly about. At my feet lay a black dog. Trying to answer a question no one could grasp, I seemed to be conversing with my wife's mother and younger brother rather coolly.

"Very quiet here."

"Anyhow quieter than Tokyo."

"Is it noisy here sometimes too?"

"This is part of the world too, you know."

And in saying so, my wife's mother laughed. True, this summer resort was part of the world. Within the past year or so I had completely come to know how many were the crimes and tragedies that occurred. A doctor who had patiently tried to kill a client with poison, an old woman who set fire to the house of an adopted couple, a lawyer who tried to dispossess his younger sister of her legacy—to look at their houses was only to see the hell of life, to me.

"There's a lunatic in this town, isn't there?"

"Perhaps you mean H. He isn't a lunatic. He's become an idiot."

"What's called dementia praecox. He always makes me feel queer. I don't know why he was bowing before the Horse-headed Kannon."

"Feel queer . . . You should be getting stronger."

"You're stronger than I am, though . . ."

My wife's younger brother, unshaven, up from sickbed, joined in, uncertainly, as always.

"I'm weak, but in a way strong . . ."

"Well, it's too bad."

Looking at this wife's mother of mine I couldn't help smiling grimly. The brother, also smiling while gazing at the pine woods beyond the fence, chattered on absent-mindedly. (The young convalescent brother sometimes seemed to me a spirit that had escaped its body.)

"I'm strangely unworldly and yet at the same time have such intense human longing . . ."

"Sometimes a good man, sometimes a bad one."

"No, something quite different from good or bad."

"Like a child living inside an adult."

"Not exactly like that. I can't say it clearly . . . Maybe more like the two poles in electricity. Anyhow I have two different things going at once."

What startled me was the roar of an airplane. In spite of myself I looked up to find an airplane flying low enough, it seemed, to graze the tops of the pines. It was an unusual monoplane with its wings painted yellow. The chickens and dog were startled too and ran about in all directions. The dog flew in under the porch barking.

"Won't that airplane fall?"

"Never . . . Do you know of any airplane disease?"

Lighting a cigar I shook my head, instead of saying "no."

"Since people riding those airplanes breathe the air of the upper atmosphere all the time, it is said that they are gradually unable to live on the air down here . . ."

Walking amidst the pines whose branches never stirred even once after I left my wife's mother's house, I found myself little by little depressed. Why did that airplane take that course, just over me, and not another? Why did they only have Airship cigarettes at that hotel? I wrestled with these various questions and walked on streets chosen for having no signs of life on them.

The sea was gray and clouded over beyond a low sandhill. On the sandy shore stood the frame of a swing without a swing on it. Looking at it brought immediately to mind a gallows. And a few crows lit upon it. They all looked at me, but showed no sign of taking wing. And one crow, in the center, lifted its beak to the sky and crowed four times.

Walking along the strand with its withered grass, I decided to turn off along a path where many villas were located. To the right of the path was supposed to be a two-storied wooden Western-style house, standing white among high pines. (A good friend of mine called it "The Abode of Spring.") But in passing it I noticed only a bathtub on a concrete base. A fire—quickly came to mind and I walked straight on, trying not to look in. A man on a bicycle was coming straight on. Wearing a dark brown hunting cap, his eyes oddly fixed, hunched over the handles. Unexpectedly I felt my older sister's husband's face on his face and decided to turn off up a lane before he reached me. But in the center of the lane lay, on its back, the dead body of a mole.

That something was aiming at me began to make me with each step more uneasy. Half-transparent cogs gradually began to block my view. Fearful that my last moment was finally at hand, I walked on and kept my neck rigid. As the cogs increased in number, they began also to turn. At the same time the pine wood on my right began to seem as if seen through fine cut glass with the branches quietly intertwining. I felt my heart throbbing and tried many times to pause on the path. But it wasn't easy even to pause, as if I were being pushed on by someone . . .

After about thirty minutes I was upstairs resting on my back and suffering from an acute headache, my eyes firmly closed. Then, from behind my eyelids a wing of overlapping silver feathers like scales began to appear. It was clearly reflected upon my retina. Opening my eyes, I looked up at the celing and having confirmed that there was no such thing there, decided to close my eyes again. But the silver wing as surely returned with the darkness as before. Then I remembered, there had been a wing too on the radiator cap of the cab I took the other day . . .

Someone came up the stairs hurriedly and ran down soon after with a clatter. Startled at realizing it was someone's wife, I immediately got up and went down to the dark living room that the stairs led to. My wife, who seemed to be suffering from shortness of breath, resting upon her face, was trembling at the shoulders.

"What's the matter?"

"No, nothing . . ."

Finally she lifted her face and forced a smile while talking.

"Nothing—it just came into my mind, Father, you were about to die . . ."

It was the most frightening experience in my life—I haven't the strength to go on writing. It is inexpressibly painful to live in such a frame of mind. Isn't there anyone to come and strangle me quietly in my sleep?

NOTES

[1] The Tokaido Line is famed in the prints of Hiroshige and by the modern bullet train—the main railway link between Tokyo and Osaka.

[2] A *furoshiki* is a large square of cloth still very much in use in Japan to carry bundles in, etc.

[3] A *hibachi* is a ceramic, or sometimes wooden or rock, brazier, filled with sand and holding small chunks of charcoal. It is still common in the hinterlands and along the fringes of life in Japan.

[4] The *basho* tree, from which the famed haiku poet took his name, is the plantain.

[5] Maruzen is the best-known book chainstore in Japan—even yet.

[6] *Anya-koro* ("Journey into the Dark," 1912–37) is the best-known novel of Shiga Naoya. Akutagawa, who had almost entirely given himself to writing about ancient scenes, etc., in his final year or so felt moved by his more autobiographically oriented contemporaries to explore his own wracked mind and body.

[7] The monument to Shushunsui was erected in 1913. A Taoist scholar and teacher, he had been invited to Japan by the Tokugawa shogunate and became a citizen in 1659.

[8] *Shakko* is the name of a periodical. The phrase "Red Light," however, should not be confused with its Western counterpart. The reference in Japanese is to the Buddhist Paradise.

SIX POEMS

CARL RAKOSI

THE VOW

Matter,
     with this look
I wed thee
       and become
thy very
      attribute.
I shall
   be thy faithful
spouse,
   true
to thy nature,
       for I love
thee
   more than Dürer
loved a seaweed.

GROUND BREAKING

If it takes almost a million years
                             for light from Andromeda
to reach a learned society

and stars sometimes explode
                         on the astronomer's time scale

and in another hundred million years
                            we shall be able to see
Maffei I,
         described as "a nearby island universe,"

then there is passion
                in the lightness of a feather,
man can hear
        his arteries hardening,
and the realist must pass
                  first through the eye of abstraction.

Yet they say it is so.

THE GLASS OF MADEIRA

Madeira,
      you have put me
into a null state.
             Now I know
what the Eskimo meant
              when he said,
"The weather is our master."

I know, you want me
                in a kind of interval
or heavy water.
           Another glass
and I'll be your placebo.

Well, I feel no pain.
                    I'll rest awhile
in this ancient limbic system.
If I sit here long enough,
                    I may figure out
the gravitational pull
                    of words:
viz., "The sea is old
                    but the earth is older."

The vine from which you came
                              was brought from Cyprus
by the Portuguese
                    to the island of Madeira
where the green canary abounds
and sixhundredninetyfive species of beetles.
The coast is rocky
                    and the sea unquiet,
hence there are few algae.
The rock is basalt
                    of volcanic origin,
dark and hard.
There are few meadows and pastures.
The cattle feed on the mountains
and on the lower slopes
                    are a few towns.
This is said
            to reassure
men of facts
            dragging an ass.

Good Madeira,
            let me lie in your glass
in the mellow quality
                    of latency.
Do not unlock us.
                The cubic light
of a small planet
                left its source
at the time of Prospero,
                    iron-red,
and entered here.

What time is this?
the axis of the earth inclines,
                                  the fish swims to the hook,
the old man plants
                 a plum tree for his granddaughter.

Profound Madeira,
                 let me get some of this pressure
off my bladder.
                 I'm stoned.
I don't know my backbone
                            from a tuning fork.
Don't any body
             bump my arm
or try to stop me

Undefinably deep and strange
                            is this lighted enclave,
this underwater amber,
like the words of a philosopher
                            with a taste for style:
"There is a mustard seed
                 in the shape of the earth.
But it doesn't matter."

In this condition
                 it is easy to be deceived.
The last words
             of Beethoven on his death bed,
after four operations, "Too late! Too late!"
also looked profound
                 until the reference was traced
to a shipment of his favorite Rhine wine.

Verily, I slobber over.
It wouldn't surprise me
                       if four mink
dashed across this scene,
                          pulling an orange crate.
I wouldn't bat an eye.

What's the matter?
Don't we peasants
                    deserve to be entertained?

I'm not going to budge
                        from this love seat
until Leah calls.

INSTRUCTIONS TO THE PLAYER

Cellist,
        easy on that bow.
Not too much weeping.

Remember that the soul
                    is easily agitated
and has a terror of shapelessness.
It will venture out
                but only to a doe's eye.

Let the sound out
            inner *misterioso*
but from a distance
                like the forest at night.

And do not forget
                the pause between.
That is the sweetest
and has the nature of infinity.

THE CHINA POLICY

Of all the old times
                    I'll take Chinese poetry.
A man could loll under a hemlock tree then
                                    and muse,

and nature be
                as wood to carpenters,
a grouse ambling by,
                        a sparrow hopping . . . .
nothing was of greater consequence . . . .
                                such sweetness flowing
as through a membrane through his limbs
                                the universe turned
into a poet's enclave,
                the great society
where simplicity is character
                        and character the common tongue,
the representative of man.

In those corrupt, bitter times
                        the most obscure clerk
could attain clarity
                from these poems,
and his nature,
and change into a superior man
                        of exquisite modesty
by simply looking at a heron crossing a stream.

CENOZOIC TIME

A man looks
        at a rock.
The rock sits.
                Rock and man.
The rock is.
        What is being?

He has sensed his nature,
idea as idea,
and trembles
before the insoluble art.

BRAIN CELL 9,999,999,999

PAUL WEST

Howdy-do, April 23rd 1616. Don't answer: I never have long, am always on call, like the fire brigade, interrupted or left to my own low-keyed devices. It's dark in here, with occasional fireworks that shoot clean through me, on their way to—where I never know. One of the Many (ten billion of us: same population as Mondo Novo, Cathay, and Ind combined), I rarely can espy the One as a whole, although my stock of rumors and debris grows. I'm a nonstop gossiping *child* who amasses a collection of broken eggshells. One day I'll become a cortical pyramid, oh what dizzy heights of social climbing!, fragile but flawless uniform dove-gray; until then, I stick to my last (as they say on the outside), picking at the walls of this, you guessed it, field-gray cell. Powerful-seeming, we boast at maximum ten watts, not very bright, and my everyday experience is becoming unbearable: just *imagine* (what a tactless word to use!) ten billion souls all on top of one another in this spherical reserve, as if we were Indians. Mice go mad under such conditions, cannibal or schizophrenic, so why not ourselves? Why not I? As it is, the mob prevails; feuds and alliances, purges and *coups d'état,* happen in a millisecond, and here more than anywhere else no one is an island. The main is all. I'm always vulnerable. My property isn't mine. I'm forever quiescent or excited. I can't keep up. And even what I'm doing now—talking back or thinking counter—isn't allowed, although how punished I know not. Soon, presumably, I'll find out.

The lull continues, condition Alpha, Alf for short (whereas Meg, or Omega, is a sunburst); so I'll resume, do my best. At day's end, like a kelp forester, I often relax mentally by roaming, just as mentally of course, through the upper branches of the forests that enclose me. Creatures weird and exquisite swarm about me, jellies and reefs and vinelike streamers, quite blocking the wattlight with their tangle. I need no— sorry, there was a rush on just then. A red-hot front coursed through, which means He thought intensely while dreaming. A night-Meg prevailed, speeding me up from, oh, ten twitches per second to hundreds, nay thousands. *He* is mine host. As I was saying, I need no wings or swim-fins; I live vicariously, combing the beach of this Mind or, at whim, flying, swimming, or even cycling. Poaching's the favorite local sport; after all, some of us, at our extremities, are only 200 angstrom units apart, which is to say we don't overlap only a bit more than we do, so it's downright impractical (not to say uncivil) to tell someone to get off your doorstep. Indeed, the smallest of us, the infant oilcan-bearers, are so tiny that it cannot be known, over a period as brief as the afore-said millisecond, where they are. The more you know their speed, the *less* you know where they are, in fact, and the more you think you know where they are or aren't, the less you know about their speed. Very wearying if you value friendship, as I do. That sort of thing may well one day become a big discovery on the outside; in here it's commonplace. It stands to reason, I suppose; I keep saying that, but Reason's quite mythical to me, part-object of a local cult.

I've been in here, I estimate, since your Aprilian 23rd of 1564, when mine host (traditionally speaking) switched on, puling and passing all beneath him, which was the time of the Great Long Alf: much fuss, yes, but just as much repose and coma. If I'd been a creative type, it's in those years I'd have zoomed. As it is now, His demands are colossal (he even sleeps energetically), and I have hardly even time for such an avocational voluntary as this. Let him thank his lucky stars we only improve with use—why, I have several grossly overdeveloped synaptic knobs, each nearer to sister- and brother-knobs than is decent, each a-swill with the notion-fluid which is to the engram what foreplay lubricants are to sperms (one of the above-ground rumors I cherish). *Think of me,* I was on the point of saying, *as an encrusted tree branch,* but I withdraw that fallacy: one of my abiding problems is comparison, into which

I'm often tempted. Truth told, our—no, *my*—experience is unique; and all comparisons deform it. So I am not, although I resemble these, a tollbooth on a six-lane highway, although that is close; or the baby-carriage lurching down the Odessa steps in the movie called *Battleship Potemkin*, although that is dynamically more accurate; or, for that, the copper flange in the chest of a flashlight, although that likeness in its care for volition is almost on the ball. If these flashes-forward bewilder you, the fault is hardly mine. Mine host is forward-looking, like Leonardo da Vinci, whom I wish were my uncle. Hardy mote, I exist between the fact and the hypothesis, deep in a maelstrom of millions of neuronal inter-actions, some of them futile, some immortal. I personally receive from one hundred neighbors, and transmit to as many more. "The neighborhood fence?" you ask. Well, if you must get metaphorical, which is no doubt understandable for a designated day in April, yes; except, in here, in the ghetto, we don't play on words; words play on us, and He on them.

That much uttered, by way of introductory (a handshake be-fore firing), I want to record my own part, for posterity of course, in perhaps the gravest crisis mine host had, I pitching my idiom forward in the guessed-at future. Minor I may have been, like a Western Union boy in the Pentagon, but major the consequences were, as I've discovered by putting together in spare time (while He slept, as now) a trillion different intuitions filched from, or accidentally shed by, idling neighbors. See how engrammatically I speak! Believe it or not, but just remember (and here I address myself to putative peers of mine in your possession, you, April, and all Aprils to follow): I am an all-or-nothing relay; I don't always fire; I have inhibitions; I'm subject to reverberation from closed self-re-exciting chains (chains I was born in); sometimes a wad leaps through me, and a hundred thousand like me, right on to the massive bridge of pulp in the corpus callosum (locally known as the Bridge of Lies), thus activating the other hemisphere of the brain, dipping through the white matter to set up a new excitatory focus a long way off. Citizen therefore of two hemispheres, I'm worldly enough for this. And, considering all the static I'm subject to from funnybones bumped and the intemperate consumption of sack, etc., I merit a hearing. All of us in his knowledge, in our knowledge of Him, are secret sharers. So curb your intoxication with surfing on wavefronts as they curve and loop through a multitude of nets. And hear this:

Well into it, just past the three-hundredth line of his twenty-second play, mine host struck both gold and trouble during a summer afternoon in 1601, when the sweat of his wrist and arm dunwetted the page on which he wrote. (Thanks to massive assists from us he composed in enormous long bursts, never blotting a line save with his arm.) In full cry he came up with, *via* us, I insist, the combo well-known as *O, that this too too,* and stopped cold. Notice the repetition often slanderously ascribed to a double-firing synapse, as the jargon of the neurologists is going to have it. My first datum, as the breaker swamped me after a whole series of fringe-captures and coalescings, was of pressure on a certain area of skin, up there beyond the periscope; then of this's interacting with wavefronts that signaled muscle-sensation and warmth. The result: something massy, tensed-smooth, and warm. Perhaps it was a sense of swollen udder on a cow, but *we* never know: integration of data occurs between wavefronts generated by the most diverse receptor-organ discharges from eye and hand, or from eye and ear, or discharges from the retina, the eye-, neck-, and body-muscles, et cetera, all set adventuring among the memory bank of already congealed engrams. Ugh. What a shambles. Pity us middlemen, do.

Nonetheless, candidate number one was *sluggish:* evoking terrestrial gastropod molluscs, or smooth soft larvae. Already mine host had leaped ahead to *flesh* (his walking is a series of recovered falls), the flesh being more of a problem to him than to us, or to me, and he began stirring up the circuitry that would dump *sluggish's* rivals. After all, he was somewhat dazed by the heat of that unusual summer, as well as weary after three hours and twenty-two minutes of writing, and, to be candid, a bit hostile to flesh after a recent dose of the Neapolitan boneache. *Sluggish* would do, being lazy, little-human, and a whit repulsive. It would distance the flesh. *Too* tapped its foot twice while, yonder, *flesh* waited in the wings, parentheses between two worlds, one doubled, the other waiting to be turned. But then *slug* grew fat and hot, exploded into ocher carrion for the region's kites and afternoon London dogs, and waves began advancing toward me at indescribable speed on several fronts. I reproduce that plenty in the runways as best I can;

after all, I'm trying to elasticize a pinpoint flash. Will you settle for a wiring-plan of the engram itself?

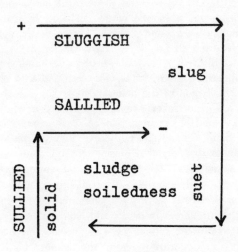

Faster than *suet* liquefied into *sludge*, the *soiledness* of *sludge* triggered (it *was* that abrupt) the metathesized form *solid*, which mine host, averse to double decompositions, at once rejected, his mind seething with how too, too often his *solid* flesh had *sallied* forth liquidly only to return home *sludge-sullied* and *sluggish*, which was the number he had first thought of. Imagine the claustrophobia in here! Ugh-huh.

And so to bed? Did he lock *sallied* home forevermore to be? Not quite. Mine host habitually pens, in his "English" hand, his *a* with the rear loop left unclosed, and therefore he set down on this occasion, as usual, but with a sigh of relief so total it sounded as if he had expired, what looked like a *u*. Hence, *sullied* for *sallied*: no fault of mine: I inhabit an enchanted loom where millions of flashing shuttles weave a dissolving pattern, always meant to be "meaningful," though never an abiding one; a shifting harmony of subpatterns. I'm not commercial, am not in trade, am not obliged to deliver the goods. So the fault, if fault there be, lies with another part of the loom—the motoric switches no doubt—as well as with mine host's own sloven nature. Daedal anonym that I am, I serve, I witness, have no license-to-deplore. Understandably, then, I sometimes, rather shortcircuitedly-minded, wish along with Him, O, that *this* too too (   ) would as well. . . .

But not often. To resume: he didn't even mumble *eureka!* (I have found it!), which specific grave idiom I received vicariously. Rather than his having found it, it had found him, found him wanting, and couldn't speak on its own behalf. Mine host wrote down his line and then forgot it, which is to say that its multiple representation in the cortex—that loaded mushroom of gray fiber .1 inch thick and 400 square inches in area which forms the deep-folded surface of our twin hemispheres—wasn't enough. I mean (it often happens) that most of my neighbor neurons lost it while I retained it (being in the minority, so to speak), whereas some that I lost others retained. You can't win them all. It's all, I reckon, a matter of spike potential, depends on how readily you respond to a single excitatory synaptic impulse, which I privately think of as having a noetic erection all the way on the graph from −70 to +20 millivolts. Some quicken and endure longer than others do; I mean some quicken faster and endure longer. . . . I, number 9,999,999,999 (or so I surmise), I the penultimate neuron and almost the last word am one of fortune's favored, at least when I contrast myself with vicinals in here: castrati, eunuchs-born, prem.-ejackers, hang-nail-membered, not forgetting those truly impotent ones in love with the Dura Mater (the hard braincap up on high who keeps us all under) or those annulled for keeps by alcohol. Forgive me, April 23rd, 1616, I *am* addressing you, but sometimes you feel like the world at large and all of time as well; like posterity in volume.

What fidgets me most is the chance of this's being a wasted record, a fond, daft, merely mutinous thing due to erase itself around May 1616, only next month (a majority vote of seven tenths of all eligible neurons having decided this). True, I may survive through connotation, or quotation even, as if some fellow or sub-host in ages hence might approach *O.t.t.t.t.s.f.* with a cerebrality fierce enough to divine my brittle solo song behind it. Or, if not an entire sub-host or fellow, or not even a complete loom, then some eerily empathetic cell, sick of serving but lovesick, and avid to travel through time. That there will be no transplants before (or even long after) next month, I am certain; that telepathy, or the introduction into craniums of changeling dreams, will postdate my end (at least as sanctioned -ologies), I am clear. But cheep on I do, chirp-chirrup, hoping against hope that what I sense coming up here from down there isn't the beginning tremor of mine host's eviction, and thus inevitably of mine. God help us, he wakes! He burns alive! Someone tell him please: *I* am the host, *he's* the dependent one. In the beginning I was his child, but now I'm one of his many fathers. It's *his* flesh must melt, so be it, but (responsibly thinking) I'm not flesh at all; and so, when (while) he goes the full distance, achieves his corpse, thawing and resolving himself into a dew of marsh gas, *I* am the Everlasting, distilled from a billion trillion echoes. Those words, those lines, that line of lines, that sixty-five-thousand-dollar subjunctive beginning *O*, oh those are my flesh. So while the line endures, on live I. Mine ex-host redounds with redundancy. I, Cell 9,999,999,999, am the ghost of Hamlet Junior's sixteenth line (I use the quarto of 1604–5 and the projective effort of counting up the lines almost finished me). So long as men shall live, or eyes see, so long live I, ghostly Sadducee. Surely one day my encomiast will come, see behind the line to its only surviving witness, who's survived even the line's corrupted willed-on funk.

Yet a tympany down there, preluding a thunder fit to panic a billion cells up here in the attic, gives me pause. 'Tis more than merely his waking up, being some trauma: either on a vast scale the neuronal counterpart of a problem clamoring for solution (e.g., how to start *The Tempest*, which got us all seasick, whereas *sallied-sullied* affected just a few, mainly me) or—catch my breath—*finis* to mine host's incessantly weaving the spatio-temporal patterns of his beloved engrams into those continually novel and interacting forms immortalized as brain's children, Mind's *Kinder*. What an ague is here! He wakes, only to know he dies, and has to do it now. Beaumont's gone already; Cervantes too. *Kindertotenlieder?* Child-death-songs? No, not yet. Let me be born, out of this womby Auschwitz. Oh, please. I penultimate an ultimatum make: the billionth cell's a ghost. I stalk. It must be so. One always gets away, even a Mohican. Our Will is fat and scant of breath. Our Will was made this March. Otherwise, to be literal, phew, sometime in August 1563. The superior man rights the calendar. But to be born, however traditionally, on a 23rd, and on another 23rd to have to . . . that's too much. Alpha. Bravo. Charlie. Delta. Not this thunderous rending. Behold: The Engrammarian at last! No Folio till 1623? Again the 23! 23 x 3. Lemmings all amelt. *Eureka!* Choking. Black. Gray. Whi . . . Mine Host, O Mega O

THREE POEMS

ROBERTO SANESI

Translated by William Alexander

LETTER TO YEWROLINSKIJ

> *The problem of time and poetry in the body*
> *of reality is like a mole; even if it sometimes*
> *emerges, it cannot see the light.*

Other laws. Diverse. The logic of time,
    the technical knowledge
of its conditioned truth, of an innate thesis
that evades chronicle, place and atmosphere
with geometry's rigorous wisdom. Diverse
in their repetition of an exact,
    uncontrollable fact,
                diverse,
declared in the void, recorded and dead,
as in autumn the leaves take on
a design of new annunciation,
    a maturity the eyes
sustain in silence.

And in this night that sweats a wind
of heavy mist (the careless account
of rumpled sheets, of bodies etched
in the bed, of sleep, of anxiety that seizes you
where theater does not close the gold
and sepia shade of the horse chestnuts) you lie awake,
listening, stretched out in a room to share
the spiteful fables of contemporaries:
with that vain insistence that limits the object
to an image or norm of thought.
                                        Recall
how the horizon sky stretches
when light meets the apex
of a sparrow's flight and settles where
a wall sustains an unknowable face of stone,
an ex-voto of time; how in the eyes
condenses the light that repeats
and proposes again the blood of an open hand
if you watch the slight edge of the fingers;
or how an aged creeper's naked fiber will suffice
to spread the light beyond the fleeting life
allowed to it.
                In its significance,
eternity bestirs itself, word, in an abstract November,
not thinking at all of the irony of a virile gesture,
of what you call fate and is merely history.
                                        And here
of values I do not speak:
                        the theory of time—if I watch
a shadow stir on the damp asphalt
in the anguish of browns, I see no solitudes
but a firm and simple step—and all its laws
have a lugubrious calling, an unsteady
verbal world, a method perfect
for control: your inexperience
guarantees whatever is declared.
                                If you wish,
the possible synthetic perceptions,

even the real concordances—your body opposite you
who say I think, your body an object viewed
or visible; or think—your body that thinks
your thought—of deeds in terms of value,
or of gestures wherein you sink: if you wish,
such degradation you can always attain:
INSPECTIO SUI, as those who know affirm.
                                    For which
you must run the risk: this is the poetry
that I can dedicate to you, a dubious
physiognomy of many latitudes which sinks
in a perpetual mockery. And then
in the instant aridity of an internal upset
emerges the sound of horse chestnut husks that explode
and touch the earth with a weight of precarious life,
the night grows gigantic in the velvet cavity—
you reject the (partial) content: emotional intrusion:
a carbonaceous nude observing you
from the window.
                    At this point, it seems to me,
you drew a circle inside a circle on the vacant page,
then slowly copied it again with a light slant,
repeated, obsessive, while the leaves gave off
a pungent color of putrefaction, and the circle vanished
beyond the low edges of the page. This was your right
to reach the point—and perhaps obscurely—
of declaring yourself multiform and unique.
                                    (At dawn
the shadows bend slowly over the first infancy
of an open window.)
                    Deep distraction,
order inpenetrable: within you hide
nebulous places, you trace yourself
in a fragment of glass and respond to yourself,
reflect yourself, and suddenly see yourself
and remain unsure. Touch yourself.
                                The problem
is only one of language: an astute recovery
at the moment of impossible choice.

(1966)

FOLLOWING THE TRADITION OF PANTOMIME, BEFORE THE CURTAIN IS RAISED ONE OF THE CHARACTERS PRESENTS HIMSELF TO THE PUBLIC.

thought, when it questions itself, cannot cease to continue and to contradict itself, but there is a thought in action, and it is of this that one must give account*

The correct inclination of the brow
on the arm, thinking, or like
one who thinks
        (logic: a word
within another word, within
another word)
           to flee from himself to one
who recalls him to impossible likenesses;
                     I remember:
I sat beneath an imaginary tree
in contemplation of the Acheron,
                a match
kindled between my fingers in a January averse
to the strict harmonies of the snow, nebulous;

and you should have seen how (silent, from above)
    they whirled or stretched
with quick spurts in a determined line
to find a form and begin, to arrange
a start, to decide not a phrase
but a fact, an idea, a blue
glass that cuts and is changed
into the vocalism of things,
an object (anti-expressive function of what
its own nature confirms), or, better still,
a grimace to recompose.

* This epigraph, in the original Italian, is a marginal gloss for lines 6–13.

                    I know: what does not change
is always this frenzied,
                    violent,
                            silent
desire to change, and its color is a white
charged with emotion and organized in rhythms,
        as if it were, and as
        it often actually is—
        this projection of ourselves—
        but a false introspection
        repeated to the limits of a language
        that expropriates what you
        call reality.
                    And I, again: we:
body growing old anxiously mute,
the cheeks withered, the skin
tight at the temples
                        (the remnants of the body nails hair
burn without odor) and IN A DREAM I LOST
        MY TEETH, I SPIT
    THEM IN A HAND, WITHOUT GRIEF,
        COLORED AND SHINING. Yes,
    sometimes I also rend myself. Forms,
    disconnected deformities. And he made (for them)
    a garment of beauty. Worn out.

                ·   ·   ·

Seated perhaps a bit snobbishly with a cloak
of nocturnal velvet I now pretend to act
a time from a play (see *Sprechmelodie*,
where death continually pierces my throat,
confounding me, a part
for a single character), but what I do
I do always with all of myself.

                ·   ·   ·

The correct inclination of the brow
on the arm—and it is not to corrupt,
but to gauge non-being and return to meaning—
that nothing may move you, that you may avoid pity,
anguishless vagabond poisoning wells
of private dialects; but it is not . . .
                              (And thus
even pride suffocates.)
                        I: circumscribed.
From the window the roofs (the rain) certainly not
the kingfishers, the blackbirds, nor, even less,
the wrens or the birds of paradise, those
you wanted to hear: *kee-kee*
in the trees, and slender antennae, the light
oblique with the weight of clouds, and in the mouth
a taste of seeds, which I chew, and in the eyes—see,
I hold them open—a vision whose contours
I do not exactly grasp.

(1967)

ELEGY FOR VERNON WATKINS

You would have said that the hills of Wales
were lilac and green in the arid wind
of the ferns and the sea, the harebells and horses
riding the clouds, the herons and gulls
pell-mell in the air like white petals,
and you would have surrendered
to the repeated sound, subdued, glittering
from the mirroring sky of the concave moon
saying to yourself this sand, this continual invisible
gesture of the wave interprets me, vision,
contemplation, silence and sound
in perfect accord like spade and soil,
clover and sickle, while you watched
from the eastern window the shadow fall
more rapidly with wide-open arms,
leaving the seashell the final light
and ultimate wound, holly
of the memory, before becoming transformed
into the astounding white of the darkness.
I have let other dead withdraw serene and poised,
but only when death had come and only to us,
let them withdraw in their certainty
their deceit was not revealed by us. Yet you
truly saw the birds' golden eyes
fixed in a Word of diaphanous waters, the air
an undulant column of meanings
stretched from an unmoving butterfly
to a mystery closed in the butterfly's wings. And then
you decline compassion, you are fulfilled
and return, seeking within the crystal sphere
you hold smiling in your hands nothing more than its curve
and light that sail toward an October dusk. You need
no longer yield to nostalgia. Pennard recalls
your step on the sod, your nimble step that prays
to restore the solid rock and gigantic sea,

all as it should be, blood and the ear of corn
in league with your step and breath. I see you
at tennis with Taliesin, reversing
the Atlantic shores. You observe
the imperfect trajectory, are undistracted if asked
to trace on the court the conscious impressions
or to correct your movement by the rules of the game.
You would say the great violet night
bursting from the sunset above the Gower hills
does not contradict the cold wings of the swan
attending its path. By instinct you knew
that conjecture will never be able to lead
to a true equation: you come back perhaps
completely for this. You knew how to adapt
your partial vision to the limitation of time,
you brought the sense of your vision
into the astounding white of the darkness.

(December, 1967)

WEDDING FINGER

JAMES PURDY

Saint-Stephen comes out on a bare stage, wiping his wings free of imperfections.

SAINT-STEPHEN. I am a child of the bluegrass region of our big continent, viz., Kentucky. I have not found happiness in New York. Nonetheless, the bluegrass has changed so much (I am informed), I cannot go back there either. So I am as it has been diagnosed by somebody or other (my memory is terrible nowadays), diagnosed as a day-to-day orphan with indecipherable mental lapses. In Kentucky I lived in a tissue-paper colored pillared house you might call porticoed. I had melancholy then, but not the incurable type I'm afflicted with now, and when it came on unduly, all I had to do was walk out into the bluegrass and clap my hands.

SPECTATOR (*who also plays the role of the black servant*). Why, that must have been a clean century ago!

SAINT-STEPHEN. In less time than it takes a kite to be caught in the branches of a telephone pole, a servant in a Palm Beach suit of the male sex would approach me, and say:

CATO. Master Stephen, does you have the vapors again so early in the A.M.?

SPECTATOR. Stop that shameful darky spiel, halt it!

SAINT-STEPHEN. And I would reply, Cato (or Julius, if Julius was able to get up that day), Cato, I have the misery so early this A.M., and I wonder if you would maybe soothe me till it passes.

CATO. Well, Master Stephen.

SPECTATOR. This is criminal backtracking. I say, jump off there!

SAINT-STEPHEN (*to Spectator*). You piss off there, you knot me up like.

CATO. Master Stephen, there be a lot of bluegrass to cut this A.M.

SAINT-STEPHEN. Do you mean I'll have to give out one of my commands, Cato? Oh, I am boiling! Mad as a farm of hornets! My ribs are rattling with rage.

CATO. Well, wait till I put away my scythe, young 'un. (*Cato picks up Saint-Stephen and carries him to a big rocking chair, and as he rocks him he sings some unrecognizable blues number.*) Master Stephen, you done covered me with your salt tears until I am a drawn tub bath, and I got to go into the big house and find four to six Turkish bath-size towels to dry myself off.

SAINT-STEPHEN. Don't leave, Cato, baby. I was just getting to feel comfortable in your capable hands.

CATO. But I be drippin' from all your weepin', master. . . .

SAINT-STEPHEN. I'll dry you off with a catalpa leaf, if you'll stick.

CATO. Never in your life, Master Stephen. No leaf will do that. I'm dripping soaking wringing wet. (*Cato slowly disengages himself from Saint-Stephen and more slowly ambles toward the big house.*)

SAINT-STEPHEN. I know you. You won't be back. Wherever I ever needed somebody, they lit out, and never did come back. Well . . . somebody in the big house will want him to rock them too. That's the way it goes. (*Music tells the audience Saint-Stephen is back in New York.*) That's the way it is today. I need somebody even more desperately but nobody comes near. Nobody comes. . . . So that was how I was melancholy in Kentucky. (*He claps his hands violently, rushing about the stage as he does so.*) You hear that, Spectator. When I clap now, nobody comes at all. Not even a stray pigeon. That is what's choking me.

SPECTATOR. Rot-gut! Pussy! Bad-ass! Lickdish!

(*Saint-Stephen weeps violently and sits down in a new chair, rubbing his fists in his eyes like a small child.*

(*Lights go out. When they come on again, Saint-Stephen has recovered, is in a riding-habit, with brightly bedizened buggy whip held in hand.*)

SAINT-STEPHEN. Because I am suffering from a disease which has no diagnosis, let alone cure, the World Manager of All-Seeing Lenses has asked me to present before you the Electric Mirror of the Cosmic Universe. It is a story too precious to lose in the cobwebby archives of peripheral history. I will therefore (*he takes out a giant lens to the spectators*) serve as *narrator superfluous* and introducer of (*he claps his hands violently*) One, The Cannibal Prince (*who comes forward and bows*), Two, Lady Tuttle (*she comes forward*), and Three, Her venerable versatile distinguished Lady Mother, Minnie Mae (*she comes very near to the footlights*), and Four, the Great Evangelist Obadiah Greethurst (*he acts like a boxer, holding up his arms and grinning and making coughing sounds*). Silence, Obadiah, no preaching or using any form of lighted tobacco here . . . I should add for the comfort of our spectators that all these persons are legally dead. They come to us through the courtesy of our neighbor the Marble Pillar Cemetery and its custodial Raven, which is willing to allow these honored dead to appear through the Great Opera Glass invention which I still hold in my hand (*he shows again the giant lens*), a sort of Cosmic Eye, I am told, which allows the human brain to travel backward through the burial of history, whose real name of course you remember to be Clio. I myself, I see you are already asking, am I among the quick or the passed-over dead? Guess my secret, *messieurs et dames*. (*Laughs maniacally*) You may call me, however, a nigger-kisser.

SPECTATOR. This be no bona fide Saint-Stephen, the proto-martyr. This be the notorious gambler, hashish-sucker Tim Luter, of Cowick, Kentucky, who earns his keep by selling young men into white slavery on coffee boats, never to be heard of again by their friends or fambly. Listen to any Missing Persons Bureau broadcast on your radio hour.

SAINT-STEPHEN. And which of those young men you claim I sold onto the coffee boats ever so much as sent back one post card of complaint concerning their voyage to Rio? Answer my question, smart-eyes. . . . You see (*to the audience*) he has no sincerity. These youths he pretends to pity—he would like to join them, and has asked me not once but a hundred or thousand times to let him be shanghaied to some similar destination. He too desires aristocratic lodgings with a backdrop of painless sin and a lover of his own dimension . . . Kneel! (*He forces the Spectator down.*) I say, all the way down . . . Now start kissin'. (*Spectator kisses the feet of Saint-Stephen.*) More thorough! Suds those old clodhoppers. . . . Dismissed. (*Sits down exhausted*) This disciplining of my characters wilts me like a line of dish rags. I am bushed. . . . Oh it's so hard to make anyone behave. (*He jumps up to kick the departing Spectator on his behind.*)

SPECTATOR (*from the audience*). Just the same, this here Saint-Stephen ain't no saint. He is living in sin at this very moment with a vicious criminal name of Loman Cogges, twice convicted, always escaped from custody, wanted in eighty-two counties on the same old charge. He no holy man, nor no actor. His white lead make-up, do it fool one mother's son soul?

LADY TUTTLE (*stepping forward*). Get on with this damned request show. I'm expected up town. I am getting never a red cent for appearing here in carnival. I'm an uptown woman, and you can just step on it. Stephen! start your rigmarole, and don't you dare take off that white paint. (*To the Spectator*) And you go back to the man who is keeping you. I know a kept youth when I see one. . . . Come out now, and let's begin (*she calls with her head thrown back*).

(*Enter Prince Antelope*)

LADY TUTTLE. Prince Antelope, *messieurs et dames*. A big hand here. Prince Antelope is one of the first modern men who has been able to soul-merge with beasts and birds, and speak their language uninterrupted with them. . . . (*To Stephen*) Do him up brown now. I'm going off to have my black eye treated.

SAINT-STEPHEN. Oh, Prince Antelope, are you on next. . . . I haven't prepared my rigmarole. (*Hunting in a large carpetbag for his notes; from it fall many flowers, mostly geraniums, violets, and big red roses. At last he finds a sheaf of papers, and begins sorting through them. Then he puts on immense spectacles. Begins reading.*) You have indeed, Prince Antelope, conversed with beasts and birds in all countries round the globe, are about to publish your experiences in a book titled *Out of My Mouth and Theirs*.

PRINCE ANTELOPE. Ahem.

SAINT-STEPHEN. A large audience is eagerly waiting to hear of your phenomenal experiences, and I wonder if you could tell us just how you began to realize that you could soul-merge and converse with the unexplored outdoors.

PRINCE ANTELOPE. Well, a few years after I was born in Haiti, I realized that men did not have the wherewithal to continue as a real going concern. . . .

SAINT-STEPHEN. Begging your pardon, Prince Antelope, but your curriculum vitae here states you were born in Africa. But you say it is Haiti?

PRINCE ANTELOPE. I born in Africa but left for Haiti in a boat the same week.

SAINT-STEPHEN. Yes.

PRINCE ANTELOPE. As I say, I was seeing no sense in continuing with the human institution when as astrology teach, they is in their last cycle here under the sign of Pisces, and the Forces tell me I should go get next to the birds and the beasts, the so-called Lower Kingdom, follow? On account of the Lower Kingdom is the one going to inherit the terrestrial planet on account of the men people having disappointed the Creator for the last time. So I begin going out with the beasts and birds and soul-commingled.

SAINT-STEPHEN. How old were you when the mission was made clear to you by what you call the "Forces"?

PRINCE ANTELOPE. I was ten going on nine.

SAINT-STEPHEN. Ten going on eleven?

PRINCE ANTELOPE. Going on nine. You see, we are going backward now in cyclic time, so I was getting younger even when I was growing up.

SAINT-STEPHEN. Yes. And then what happened?

PRINCE ANTELOPE. I began with a lion. I had not thought this out, mind you, but I was walking in a sandy desert and he come out of his house and called to me. I immediately allowed my soul to leave my body and go over to his and commune. He waited just a little while still looking at my human body and then his soul left his body and communed with mine. (*During this speech a lion has come out of the wings, and goes through the aforementioned motions.*) After that all lions was my friend.

SAINT-STEPHEN. How did you feel when contact had been established—your soul with his soul?

PRINCE ANTELOPE. I felt his soul-envelope pervade over me, thicklike. I merged with him as we allowed our soul-breath to come out of us.

SAINT-STEPHEN. Now when you were establishing contact with this lion, did you make sounds like words or did your communications limit themselves to his soul-air contact flowing out of you and over each of you?

PRINCE ANTELOPE. Words, too. The beasts and the feathered creatures too did utter words which through my prior studies each of us comprehended.

SAINT-STEPHEN. But another, ordinary man standing nearby would not understand what you and the beasts and as you say feathered creatures said to one another.

PRINCE ANTELOPE. That's so.

SAINT-STEPHEN. But what would they say to you, translated, as it were, into human language?

PRINCE-ANTELOPE. They all agreed on one thing. I was to go and marry with the Island of Manhattan and having espoused her, was to tow her back as my bride to where human kind first drew breath, viz., Africa, for once the world was free of this island, creation could begin all over again.

SAINT-STEPHEN. And this is your mission here today?

PRINCE ANTELOPE. It be.

SAINT-STEPHEN. Roughly how many beasts have you communed or souled with?

PRINCE ANTELOPE. Roughly?

SAINT-STEPHEN. I mean, in general.

PRINCE ANTELOPE. I done lost count in general shortly after my desert experience. I met Mohammed, you know.

SAINT-STEPHEN. So I have heard.

PRINCE ANTELOPE. Where you hear it?

SAINT-STEPHEN. Why in the papers, wasn't it?

PRINCE ANTELOPE. Weren't reported in the papers. Nohow either.

SAINT-STEPHEN. Well, let's say I heard it.

PRINCE ANTELOPE. But I be telling it to you for the first time right now. This be a first.

SAINT-STEPHEN. There may be telepathy.

PRINCE ANTELOPE. Be nothing except what I tell you. Anyhow I see Mohammed walking under a date palm, and he said *Are you black Jesus?* I did not answer for a while because of his saucy tone to me. Finally, though, I thought after all he be Mohammed and older than me, so I responded, I have been with Jesus, Mohammed, for your information, but I ain't Jesus after all. Under what sign or aspect was you with him, Mohammed then queried. I cannot tell you that, Mohammed, I made answer. I am sworn to secrecy.

SAINT-STEPHEN. This was a dream or trance?

PRINCE ANTELOPE. Reality. I leave my body many times, as I done told you before you turned on the instruments to interview me with. But I am so tongue-tied from speech. I would like a frosted drink. You have a drink here?

SAINT-STEPHEN. Prince Antelope, whilst you are enjoying your drink may I comment on your rings. They are entirely out of the realm of the ordinary.

PRINCE ANTELOPE. I has cat's eye on my middle finger here. I left my carnelian ring to home.

SAINT-STEPHEN. What is your favorite gem, would you say?

PRINCE ANTELOPE. My favorite-favorite?

SAINT-STEPHEN. That.

PRINCE ANTELOPE. Let me cogitate. Emerald is apt to be blemished, though I rate her high high high. Opal too has blemishes. Now you take Carthaginian stone, a long-standing favorite of mine, as is Venus's eyelids, sometimes known to ordinary folk as love-returned or lad's love. Golden amber was a yesterday-favorite of mine, rainbow stone has thrilled me to my marrow, as has chalcedony, coral agate, moonstone, and leopard stone.

SAINT-STEPHEN. I have heard that you sometimes appear in a gown of many gems, so that you strike people as being a movie neon sign.

PRINCE ANTELOPE. I been known to appear in just about any costume. I never without a jewel somewhere. That's right. I jewel-oriented.

SAINT-STEPHEN. Prince Antelope, you came under a widespread criticism some months ago. Is this painful to you? (*He feels the Prince's forehead for temperature.*) Very well, I will continue with our interview. You were accused in a certain big old newspaper of having been the lover of the Leopard God. Is this at all a fact?

PRINCE ANTELOPE. Yes and again no as we say in astrology. I know this Leopard God, who think the sun rise and set in his own big bosom, but I did not accede to his wishes, which was that I bow down before him and worship the gravelly ground he walked on. I told him I would not do it for all the rings and gems in his diadem. I has my own future ahead.

SAINT-STEPHEN. You did not, then, as this newspaper claims, enter into soul-relationship with the Leopard God.

PRINCE ANTELOPE. Never. He offered me, like I say, a big jewel, but I said no sirree. Never have soul-relations with you, Mr. Leopard God.

SAINT-STEPHEN. Another controversial point. The present Queen of Sheba has let it be known that unless you honor your wedding engagement with her, she has no recourse but to institute proceedings against you, on the grounds you trifled with or alienated her affections, after wooing her in the Libyan Garden Desert.

PRINCE ANTELOPE. That about it, Saint-Stephen.

SAINT-STEPHEN. How did you intend to handle the eventuality of her suing you?

PRINCE ANTELOPE. I had the same trouble some few seasons past with Sheik Uaki-So-Bo, who commanded that I worship him and surrender my person to his total mercy. I extricated me from him, and I think I do so with the Queen.

SAINT-STEPHEN. I must confess I did not know there was a direct descent from, say, Bible times down to the present living Queen of Sheba.

PRINCE ANTELOPE. All I know is there she be in the Libyan Garden Desert calling herself Sheba and being called royalty likewise from everybody in the Desert.

SAINT-STEPHEN. Could you describe the present Queen?

PRINCE ANTELOPE. Well, she be about seven and a half feet tall, sunburned just on her forehead, wears a pearl hat, and has four hundred camels with school-age riders, and drinks desert date liquor.

SAINT-STEPHEN. Where does she reside?

PRINCE ANTELOPE. She has this old missionary Jesus school of the late Bethune Baker, on the edge of town, for her office. And near the palm grove, she has an old Fox Movie Palace, which she brought stone by stone from Chicago, America.

SAINT-STEPHEN. Does she believe that by marrying you she would continue her royal lineage. I mean you yourself are not of royal descent, are you?

PRINCE ANTELOPE. She claim, and I concur with her in this, that I be a descendant from Celestial Majesty.

SAINT-STEPHEN. Celestial Majesty?

PRINCE ANTELOPE. Mmm. But I be no desert man. I jungle and ocean man. I told her this when I walked the desert with her under the sign of Pisces. She say it of no account and took my hand in marriage without my noticing she had done took it at that time. She give me a stomacher of rose rubies, which I took as a gift for my good looks, not knowing it was binding as contract and that she done surreptitious put an amethyst on my wedding finger.

SAINT-STEPHEN. After you rejected the advances of the Leopard God, and the Queen of Sheba, you came by slow boat to New York City. Would you give us your impressions of the Great Metropolis?

PRINCE ANTELOPE. I be worshipped here as much as I be in the sand and desert. Even more so, I would affirm. Young men are fond of my soul-air, and want to commune in their souls with me, and I have found many ladies as tall and rich as the Queen of Sheba. I find it all as was forecast.

SAINT-STEPHEN. And now, Prince Antelope, we come to the most overwhelming section of this interview-confab. You are here, first to marry the island of Manhattan, and then to take her, in your words, "in tow," the entire island, that is, away with you. Is this not the real purpose of your visit?

PRINCE ANTELOPE. That be so. I am offering my hand in marriage to this island, under the direction of the Forces, which rule all the cosmos, and, through divine soul-breath and soul principle, we, Manhattan and I, will soon sail away together into an unknown ocean, which is above the atmo.

SAINT-STEPHEN. Wouldn't you say this passes all belief?

PRINCE ANTELOPE. Not to those of us who is in on the soul-breath principle. It inevitable, all foreseen and foretold millions of years ago.

SAINT-STEPHEN. And how will it happen when it does happen?

PRINCE ANTELOPE. After my marriage with the island, a marriage of steel and water, all the tall buildings and machines will vanish, the island will be restored to a tropical paradise inhabited only by birds and bird-people who sing but never conquer. I am the woodpecker king, it is written, and some say I be the owl king, and we will live in grace from then on forever in special green sunlight and shade. There will be no night in that time. Just dawn.

SAINT-STEPHEN. Do you have anything further to say before you are removed, Prince Antelope? (*As he says this four strong black men, one of whom holds a large cape, advance. The one holding the cape covers Prince Antelope securely in this, leaving only his mouth and nose free.*)

PRINCE ANTELOPE. There is no cause for alarm, people and gentlemen. I is here, and the arrival of my dark majesty ruling over you is sempiternal. No more good-byes, only hellos. (*The attendants roughly begin to remove him.*) Hello from the prince who loves you. Hello from the prince who recognizes you. Hello from the prince who is in you and of you and through you and beside you and with you and everywhere. Amen! Hello! Amen!

SAINT-STEPHEN (*yawning*). Good-bye, good-bye, Prince Antelope. . . . Keep him in a safe strong place, gentlemen (*to the strong-armed men removing him*). Don't let him out till we're ready for him.

(*Saint-Stephen now turns his attention to Emmeline Van Nostrand Vandervelde, known popularly by her followers as Lady Tuttle.*)

SAINT-STEPHEN. Lady Tuttle, you have advertised throughout the press of the world, including countries hitherto unknown to the popular tongue, that your hand is to be bestowed in marriage, in short that you're to be led away.

LADY TUTTLE. Alas, yes.

SAINT-STEPHEN. Is this then a fact that you are to be married?

LADY TUTTLE. Can one call it marriage at my age? I have been married forty-two times. I am tired of the very thought of there being two sexes. I long for freedom. But the laws of my island are strict. . . .

SAINT-STEPHEN. You refer to the Great Island, without which America is unthinkable according, at least, to some.

LADY TUTTLE. Heaven help me, I do.

SAINT-STEPHEN. So that you have agreed to give your hand—in marriage.

LADY TUTTLE. Yes, how many times do I have to keep telling you . . . I'm doing it for my country. Yes, they want me out of the way. I am the island, you know, my dear. America's most important island. But they want me out of the road. I've lived too long and at too high a level. America is tired of me, my dear. They feel I've grown . . . past my prime. Yet not too much so to be married! (*Angry*) When I begged them for the rest, the whole table of stockholders cried, "Marriage, Emmeline, marriage! 'Twill do you so much good. . . ." (*Whispers*) I'm to be married to a cannibal and taken to the Dark Continent, though their chambers of commerce deny it's now so called. (*Weeps bitterly*) I don't love this young man, but my hand has been put on the open market. I have no choice. I married all the others the same way. Except the thirty-eighth. He was a beautiful lad, what they call a stripling. . . .

SAINT-STEPHEN (*morosely, peevishly*). But isn't this a free country, Lady Tuttle, for Pete's sake. . . . After all, if you don't want to go to the altar you don't have to.

LADY TUTTLE. What do you know about freedom at your age? How long have you been breathing anyhow? You're twenty if you're not sixteen. . . . The most galling thing of all is freedom. The minute one is free he looks for more chains. Freedom is a kind of empty water bottle, a hole in the wall, a lapse in conversation. Did anybody ever know what to do with freedom, but to get rid of it. . . . I am destined to go on being married, married, married. I know every twist and posture of the ceremony and the ritual, and oh the first night in bed, the sobbing into the poorly laundered pillowcases, the smell of unusual armpits, the awful menace of heavy breathing, and the final husky cry of joy as he is delivered of his pent-up river. I am tired of repeating history, my dear... what saint did they tell me you were... Ah yes, Stephen.... Please loosen this bracelet, Stephen. 'Tis interfering with the circulation of blood.... I am giving myself away because my country has asked me to. I am America's richest widow-heiress, and I am this island, which America no longer loves. I am, my dear, a Name, have no fear on that score. Ask on, though the down is not vigorously growing on your upper lip. Ask and humiliate me, ask and hear damning replies. Oh, Emmeline, Emmeline, how far down you are. (*She kneels at this point, and crawls about.*) Appearing like any chorus girl for public talk! Public. Talk. Dear me, Saint-Stephen, I've gotten so common just being here. (*She weeps violently, her head in his lap.*)

SAINT-STEPHEN. Do try to compose yourself, Lady. We are facing a huge audience. May I call you Emmeline since you are so uncomposed?

LADY TUTTLE. I have always and ever faced a huge audience. My servants always witness, so to speak, my wedding night. They listened through the wee hours, as my spouse of that particular night and I tossed, turned, embraced, wept, blew our noses over the disappointment of it all. . . . Go on, question me. (*She rises now, still weeping, but less vociferously.*)

SAINT-STEPHEN. My dear Lady, or Widow, Tuttle, if you are suffering too much to continue, I need only pull this switch and we will be out of the viewing of all.

LADY TUTTLE. I don't care a straw who's watching any more. I've been sold down the river by the shareholders of America. I am this island, and I'm to be sold and float out to sea with an aborigine. Let me weep a little, before we continue the catechism. May I borrow your snot-rag.

SAINT-STEPHEN (*horrified at the word*). Lady Tuttle, mind your speech. You'll have to obey the Government rules, remember. They're watching us, they're listening, and. . . .

LADY TUTTLE. Oh, them. . . . Ask, my dear, demand, and violate. Those are the only things I've known since my early memories when as a tightly curled little girl my parents even then were thinking of my wedding night. Ask, fire away. Shoot. Do as your masters have required you to do. Don't mind Lady Tuttle.... But let me weep when I choose to weep. It's my last pleasure since they took away my table wine. At least I have some liquid refreshment from tears. You are a handsome showman and barker, Saint-Stephen. Comfort me a little. How many people are watching, did you say?

SAINT-STEPHEN. Four hundred million.

LADY TUTTLE. Considering all the trouble I've gone to to get here, it's not enough.

SAINT-STEPHEN. We are also being viewed on eight continents.

LADY TUTTLE. So.

SAINT-STEPHEN. Lady Tuttle, to return to your tragic dilemma. In order to preserve not only the environment but the cosmos itself, America has decided to allow you and your island to be towed out to sea by Prince Antelope.

LADY TUTTLE. Are you saying this for the four hundred million or informing me, merely, of what I already know?

SAINT-STEPHEN. Kindly answer the question, distinguished dame.

LADY TUTTLE. I was aware of my dilemma, of course I'm aware of it! Why shouldn't I be aware of it? It's all I have, my dilemma and my tears.

SAINT-STEPHEN. Are you unkindly disposed toward your bridegroom perchance?

LADY TUTTLE. None whatsoever. Neither am I kindly disposed. I told you all this before we went on the cosmic eye, my dear, all my marriages have been arranged by the Powers that be, I've never had any say as to who was to espouse me. And this cannibal situation is no different. They asked me of course if I was loath to cross the color line, since I am an aboriginal Indian, and they held a gun at my temple while I wrote *I am willing to go over any line the stockholders require me to.* And then I begged them to shoot me. Instead they put me in irons for two days in the Presidential Suite.

SAINT-STEPHEN. You are going beyond the program notes. Mum. Shh, and so forth.

LADY TUTTLE. I will be wondrously happy with the cannibal Prince Antelope.

SAINT-STEPHEN. And you think he will find happiness likewise with you?

LADY TUTTLE. I confess that idea had not occurred to me. Why shouldn't he be happy with Lady Tuttle? I will give him my all.

SAINT-STEPHEN. Within the next week, through the miracle of modern physics, this famous island, once owned by your people the aborigines, will be floating out to sea, never, never to be heard of again in history.

LADY TUTTLE. Yes, our destination is a large secret, though I believe Prince Antelope is better informed than I. He is a sea-going man.

SAINT-STEPHEN. You are to be married in a balloon, if I am not mistaken.

LADY TUTTLE. So I am led to understand.

SAINT-STEPHEN. Would you describe your costume for the occasion?

LADY TUTTLE. I always wear the same wedding costume, and have for hundreds of years. Feathers, and a little bunting.

SAINT-STEPHEN. Lady Tuttle, now that you are leaving, many things which were hidden before have come out into the open, so to speak.

LADY TUTTLE. I have nothing to hide. My life, if not an open book, is a kind of relief map on which I am willing to let the common folk eye my itinerary through this difficult journey under the phases of the moon.

SAINT-STEPHEN. I refer now of course to your wedding Chief Zah-ha-Lunnie.

Lady Tuttle's Hegira

LADY TUTTLE. Oh that long-ago happiness! What a terrible hankering for what seems now less substantial than a dream, but more lasting than life itself. Indeed this episode so debonairly and coolly referred to by you, for life has not dismembered you as it has me .... That time. (*She tries to remember but its insubstantiality baffles her for a while.*) Yes, now I find the thread. I had run off from my protectress. I wanted to be free to meet love unbargained for, you see. I was after all an Indian, though this, like all else of import, had been kept from me by my white upbringers. Yet finally .... (*Here Chief Zah-ha-Lunnie comes on stage.*) And at last, and in one time, my Indian soul emerged. I knew my real bridegroom could not be far.... (*The Chief approaches her quickly, and takes her in his arms.*) My chieftain appeared with his feather trimmed headgear. We walked through the forest paths. The mourning dove warned us, but we wanted only love, not safety. I went into his hogan, which is Indian for house, and like him wears feathers on its head. Here I experienced the unendurable weight of love.... It was October's golden moon. The corn and beans, squash and melons had been stored for winter fare. But in the quiet before dead winter, a great unrest arose instead of calm. Medicine Man determined I was evil, a Raven woman disguised as an Indian maid. Medicine Man commanded me to appear before the assembled council. "You have betrayed our young man!" they cried in one voice. "You must be burnt. You must die in ashes." But I bribed them, with the help of the eagle. (*Chief Zah-ha-Lunnie walks off at this moment, sorrowfully waving farewell. As he leaves, Medicine Man appears and throws a deerskin about his nakedness.*)

LADY TUTTLE (*continues*). I bribed them, Saint-Stephen, bribed them for myself, for I could not bribe them for the life of my lover. They killed him there in the forest. (*Medicine Man cuts Chief Zah-ha-Lunnie to pieces before the audience. An arm is torn off, then a leg, then the head. . . .*) I escaped only after countless dangers. Once a bear nearly carried me off. Again a mountain lion snarled and rushed at me. . . . It was now late November as I reached civilization. . . . But my arrival was more like a funeral than a homecoming. For only in the hogan of the chief had I been alive, only in the arms of an Indian. Everything since then has been walking death, sitting death, reclining death, eating death. But thank all gods at least once I was alive in his brown arms. Then I saw the embers of all the stars. Against the iron nipples of Zah-ha-Lunnie. I will meet my chief again beyond the stars. Life will begin again in the outermost of the dark.

SAINT-STEPHEN. In the Duchess of Exeter's nephew's book on you, there is a remarkable chapter titled "She Opposes Circumcision." (*A slide appears at the back of the stage showing the hideous mutilation of this savage practice.*) Would you care to make any comment on this?

LADY TUTTLE. On the chapter or on the practice?

SAINT-STEPHEN. Just as you wish.

LADY TUTTLE. I wonder if I might possibly employ for just a moment my gold toothpick which is in that little bag over there on the marble-topped table. I'm having a deal of bother with a tooth, and the dentist doesn't understand a thing about my teeth. The gold toothpick—thank you (*she receives the toothpick from Saint-Stephen, who has opened her bag*), thank you kindly. Ah! The gold toothpick was a gift from a distinguished sheik of Arabia, Felix, who hadn't, by the by, a solitary tooth in his head, but wore modeled elephant tusks cleverly capped with gold in his gums. (*During this speech she employs the toothpick with a certain savage gaucherie.*)

SAINT-STEPHEN. I gather I have broached another unwelcome subject, Lady Tuttle.

LADY TUTTLE. Oh, rubbish, Saint-Stephen. . . . But going back to the Duchess of Exeter and her pinhead nephew, and the chapter and book you have referred to, allow me to say this: I oppose surgery in general, and genital surgery in particular. Hands off there!

SAINT-STEPHEN. You oppose circumcision, good.

LADY TUTTLE. You're putting words into my mouth. But since you mention it, I oppose it, and indeed everything else called *now.* I go just as far as the Indians, and after the Indians I do not find history to my taste. After them everything gets complicated and a bit dirty. . . . If one is out in the open air and the sun and living as the gods want us to live, very little surgery is needed. And I don't believe in cutting off anything unless it is absolutely a matter of life or death. Even then, death is better. That goes for all parts of the body. Let nature have what nature gave us. In sum, yes, I oppose malodorous circumcision.

SAINT-STEPHEN. You would say then that your husbands are more men with a prepuce than without one.

LADY TUTTLE. Definitely with the prepuce! No question. If we have to choose between a slight tendency to be redolent and reek of nature, let us say, choose redolence and reek, as against surgery and chemical cleanliness, I definitely choose nature. . . .

SAINT-STEPHEN. Thank you (*but he is struck as he says this by Prince Antelope's hurling a pie at him.*)

PRINCE ANTELOPE. Stop this rot-gut talk! You hear, I'll have no more talking about my parts, no more chitchat about my marriage equipment! How long do you think I sit here and listen to be discussed like a side of beef, displayed like a carcass and bull pizzle! (*Turning to Lady Tuttle*) And you, big fat sultana, you got a ticket to paradise, and you make little faces and pretend you're giving a professor-talk on the philosophy of history. I know you and what you're like under the bedclothes. Get your jewels and paint off, hot you up a little, we'll see if any lady be left of you!

LADY TUTTLE (*laughs angrily*). Did you ever! Insulted, denigrated by one who is a master of the art of shoeblacking—in front of four hundred million dimwits. Oh, Almighty God!

(*Prince Antelope kneels down and removes her shoes*).

LADY TUTTLE. What on earth are you doing to me now!

PRINCE ANTELOPE. Putting new pumps on you, petty-pretty. (*He places glistening gold shoes with dazzling stones on her tiny feet.*)

LADY TUTTLE. No respect for my station! No memory of who I am. No meaning of anything left! Bought and sold, carried off. . . . Where is my mother?

PRINCE ANTELOPE. Is there to be a mother?

LADY TUTTLE. The world will never get rid of mothers, no matter how it tries, and don't you ever forget it, you panting brute. . . . What are you doing to me now?

PRINCE ANTELOPE (*fastening a necklace on Lady Tuttle's throat*). Take this beauteous opal necklace, and close your mouth in admiration once it's fastened on you.

(*Screams are heard from within. Lady Minnie Mae enters, dressed in sumptuous hawk feathers. She is partially blind and has difficulty seeing where she is going.*)

MINNIE MAE. My daughter! I hear her deaf contralto! My only child, where are you? I have been summoned from so far off to give you away again in holy matrimony.

PRINCE ANTELOPE (*correcting her splenetically*). Ticket to paradise.

MINNIE MAE. What a deep voice. Your bridegroom, Daughter? (*Lady Tuttle nods mournfully.*) Never before have you wed with one with so deep a voice. It reminds me of an entire lagoon of bullfrogs!

(*Prince Antelope moves off from them, and sits down on the floor in dejection, muttering "Destiny."*)

MINNIE MAE. And this ceremony is to end in the sport of hot-air ballooning. . . . Oh, the change in the times indeed! Where are you, my angel? (*She sits beside her daughter.*) We meet now only at your weddings, but I do not complain. I am living in a Divine hotel, where my every need is anticipated.

LADY TUTTLE. That is because you are dead, my dear. You have come back from the Great Beyond. (*She weeps.*) I can never get used to your being dead and always returning to give me away in marriage. . . . Oh, mothers, mothers, nothing exceeds the love of mothers!

MINNIE MAE. How many times have I prepared you for marriage, and you're still always prior to the ceremony a fountain of tears. Can't you ever be calm—as many times as you've gone to the altar.

LADY TUTTLE. Dear Mother, each time the pain is intolerable! I long so to retain my own selfhood! To be forever me! Not to give my all—to some *him!* To have some vestige of my purity! Not to lie there a repast for animal heaving lust. . . . And with him, dear heart, do you see that breathing hulk of jungle passion? He is simply foaming at the mouth to get at me! God give me strength to bear his avalanche of hot-bed consummation.

PRINCE ANTELOPE. And oh my ancestral savannahs! If as some folk say I never knew you, explain me then how I know your blood flows in my veins. . . .

MINNIE MAE. Each time by a miracle she is a virgin again before she goes to the altar. Yet I have given her away over forty-two times. I can hardly remember all her bridegrooms' names. . . . And she forgets too. . . . Her maidenhead being intact after the end of each marriage, and I being a good mother, who has studied in Proserpine's garden, must tell her life's facts. Explain the river of blood which must be crossed ere she becomes a Woman, give her herbs to make the pain and the weight less bone-crushing, for being Indian and a queen, she is thrice-removed from all this. . . . Our Catechism, my dearest darling, ho, for the forty-third or so time! . . . What do you have between your legs, my child?

LADY TUTTLE. Must I tell you in front of this universe of eyes?

MINNIE MAE. You must, you shall. . . . Where is your bridegroom?

LADY TUTTLE. Can't you smell him, if you can't see him, Mother dear?

MINNIE MAE. Ah yes (*sniffing*), mimosa, jasmine.

LADY TUTTLE. And decaying meat (*shudders*). . . . Oh darling, darling, ever the optimist, ever the refurbisher of horny nature. All right, catechize me, sweetheart. . . . Ask the impossible, and hear my ridiculous replies, my lies, my. . . .

MINNIE MAE. Did I come from the Other Shore to hear your impertinence! Who are you?

LADY TUTTLE (*solemn*). The beginning and the end.

MINNIE MAE. What is your purpose?

LADY TUTTLE. To continue the uncontinuable.

MINNIE MAE. Who do you love?

LADY TUTTLE. The man who doesn't know when to stop.

MINNIE MAE. Now, my dear, my last question in our catechism; though it is almost too simple to be asked: what do you have between your legs?

LADY TUTTLE. The river of tomorrow. . . . No more, Mother, no more. You said it was the last question. (*She weeps.*)

MINNIE MAE. There were two great experiences in my life, though it was one long floating day on water, but two remain stamped in my brain: Marriage and Death. I was married only twice, unlike my daughter, but the constellation of pain and joy never has left my mind, though I am a member of the Great Beyond.

LADY TUTTLE. I can't tell you the grief I experience knowing she is only my phantom mother. When I try to take her in my arms, she becomes like fog. She revisits me only before my greatest humiliation and anguish—when I am to be married by orders of the State. Once I escaped from them, went to a rain forest, but when I arrived. . . .

MINNIE MAE. You were only in time for your own wedding ceremony.

LADY TUTTLE. You see? Everywhere a woman goes she finds, in the end, only marriage.

MINNIE MAE. And death. Death is the great beginning. It is a marriage with the ether. I am a constellation. My eyes are fires now that see through all spaces.

PRINCE ANTELOPE. I adore the mother, I do believe, more than the daughter. (*He kneels in front of Minnie Mae.*) Ouch! She has struck me with some kind of interstellar naphtha. I am burning.

LADY TUTTLE. Learn to play your part, as I have to play mine. . . . . My mother wouldn't wipe her feet on you in any case. She was the grandest of the grand, in her time. No question of it.

PRINCE ANTELOPE. Nevertheless, I admire the mother more.

SAINT-STEPHEN (*strikes Prince Antelope with a long stick*). Resume your natural position. Who do you think is behind this, certainly not your own will power or desire. Do as you're told, do as you must do, and repeat only the lines destined for your mouth. And remove all your clothing preparatory to the wedding ceremony.

PRINCE ANTELOPE. Do I have to take off every stitch I got on in front of all and sundry?

SAINT-STEPHEN. Oh you can keep a little patch of thread here and there, I suppose.

(*Lady Tuttle averts her eyes as Prince Antelope disrobes.*)

(*Prince Antelope has beeen wearing so many robes that undressing is time-consuming indeed. He is finally seen to be [by the time he has uncovered himself down to his skin] a Christmas tree of jewels, bracelets, necklaces, lavalieres, etc.*)

MINNIE MAE. People want to be themselves, but the only freedom they find after ten thousand windings is marriage and death. They run from everything thinking they are on the way but in the end are overtaken by these two cosmic experiences. Death is the true bridegroom.

LADY TUTTLE. I eschew my mother's metaphysics, I suppose because it is true. She always philosophized, and there was nothing to do but weep when she delivered her speeches, they were so sad. She made everything so mapped-out and hopeless. In order to escape from her dicta I became married every spring, as soon as the snow was off the highest mountain. Forty-two times, as you heard.

MINNIE MAE. I begged her to be more temperate in her revolutionary energy, and not to resist the universe so perfunctorily, not to foam at the mouth over freedom. *Do not fight the universe, my dear!* But she had become an American by then, you know. Europe wasn't good enough for her, and so she and America suffer. They want everything in every orifice. Higher, higher, higher! I must have pleasure higher in every orifice. It is ending now.

LADY TUTTLE. What is ending, Mother?

MINNIE MAE (*ignoring her question*). Aha, at last he has come!

(*The Preacher has entered. He is a black man of about forty, with a barrel chest, and long hair. He wears a flowing mantle and high boots. An immense gold watch is tucked in his breast pocket, with a heavy chain.*)

PREACHER. Where are the ones who are to be joined, Minnie?

LADY TUTTLE. Why his boots are completely covered with cow ... dung!

PREACHER. Ah, Lady Tuttle's jagged contralto again! And is this hefty troglodyte the other zealot for matrimony?

PRINCE ANTELOPE. Hear you talk. Pimp! Clean your boots of that shit.

PREACHER (*opens a big book*). Just as I thought! Mismated even before the ceremony. Mismates though make the best spouses. Love don't last, but hate often does. Do you hate one another already, spouses-to-be?

LADY TUTTLE. Since you know everything, why don't you tell us.

PREACHER. I have eighteen other ceremonies to perform this morning, and I don't want none of your lip.

PRINCE ANTELOPE. You shouldn't browbeat royalty like that, Preacher.

PREACHER. Between the marriage-sheets, there's only mortar and pestle, as it was in the beginning. Nature knows no rank. . . . Now I want to see the rings to be used in this here ceremony.

PRINCE ANTELOPE. Ha, ha, you thought I wouldn't be in possession of any, now, didn't you, on account of you be a U.S. nigger.

. . . I have a whole mine of diamonds, rubies, sapphire, amethyst, mother-of-pearl, opal, topaz. . . .

LADY TUTTLE. And I have my own marriage ring, which is quite serviceable, adjudicated from my other forty-two weddings. Preacher . . . let's get on with the ceremony, whilst I have my wind . . . I know from past experience that if I first lose my wind, the connubial embrace is much more painful. (*She tries breathing in and out.*) And providence knows that with this bridegroom I need air to withstand the anguish.

PRINCE ANTELOPE. You never knew a pain in your life. Leastways not between any sheets.

MINNIE MAE. There you're wrong, Antelope. She never could stand life from the time she was handed into my arms. The sight of a worm, a crawling moth, a streamlet of red blood, a cry of someone being run over by a moving van, would send her to bed with migraine for days, even weeks. She once confessed she could not stand reality. She always suffers hideously during the wedding ritual, and coitus with a new husband is most penible to her. Most. Never deprecate another person's sufferings even when imaginary.

LADY TUTTLE. Mother always has made out I am an invalid. Yet when she crossed to the Great Beyond I managed to earn a living, somehow.

MINNIE MAE. But your style was gone. You had no one to appeal to but God, and he is of *mixed emotions,* as the press says, with regard to you. I know He feels you don't try hard enough.

LADY TUTTLE. Just the same, Mother, I earned my way after you had left me without so much as twenty guineas bequeathed to me. . . . Oh how I cried when they read me your will. *Nothing for little Lady Tuttle!* I appealed to the solicitor. *Mother left me nothing?* And he replied, *She had nothing to leave but her blessing. Wiped out clean by your husbands of the past. Wiped clean as a plate by the chief cook and bottle washer.* . . . So I married and married and married. Doctor Applegate gave me a drug which I anoint my body with and I feel no anguish (*theoretically*) from the bridegroom's embrace.

MINNIE MAE. It is so wrong to deceive and anaesthetize nature. She gets at us in another way. There is no running from cosmic agony. If you don't get it in one form it will come to you in another. No coital suffering! No consciousness the sole reality is entering your body! (*I refer to the membrum virile.*) The sole reality comes and you are unaware of its pressure? Oh, daughter, you disappoint me sometimes so profoundly.

PRINCE ANTELOPE. Guilty as crimson, all of them.

PREACHER (*to Prince Antelope*). You must put on a boiled shirt for the ceremony.

MINNIE MAE. Let him be.

PRINCE ANTELOPE (*sings*).

The enemy is coming tonight!
A shout of delight!
The Pelican will shed his blood,
And the Beetle will roll his dung.
The enemy is here in might
And blood is running like lakes;
The Pelican is winning and losing,
And the Robin Redbreast is late.

LADY TUTTLE. I can't bear it! Can't bear it. . . . Mother, Mother! Why have you left me? . . . I want to be your little girl.

MINNIE MAE. Oh, that age-old cry. That's why I put off leaving you for so long. I know your anguish. But you will face greater anguish if you do not give yourself to the bridegroom. See, he is not half bad. True, he is larger than any of your other spouses. But think of the practice you've had. Your body is ready for him, my angel. You don't think I'd allow this ceremony if I thought you weren't up to it?

PREACHER. Prepare your bodies and souls for holy matrimony, for I'm already far and behind time for my next ceremony. . . . Communicants, all stand! Stand up for Jesus! Whatever your religion! You, cannibal, stand up, just as you are, just as you will be. . . . Gimme them rings. (*He examines the rings painstakingly with an eyepiece.*) Mmmm, ahem! . . . Do you take this woman for whatever is going to happen in this world and the world to come? Look sharp, say yes. And do you, Lady Tuttle, daughter of Minnie Mae, take this here big standupfalldown for your legal wedded spouse no matter what destiny may have in store for you, and which is usually bad news for anybody who give it ten seconds thought.

LADY TUTTLE & PRINCE ANTELOPE (*in unison*). We do.

PREACHER. Then before the universal eye I here proclaim you who was two before to be one flesh. . . . Now go back there and perform the initiation into wedlock as quickly as comfort allows so me and your mother Minnie can go back to the underworld.

(*At this moment, the Hot-Air Balloon descends slowly to rear middle of stage.*)

LADY TUTTLE. Oh ye gods, ye gods!

PRINCE ANTELOPE. Come into my capable hands. (*He ushers her into a small chair in the balloon, and begins unbuttoning. Shortly he makes movements as of one entering her private parts.*)

LADY TUTTLE. Oh, God Almighty, I am being impaled!

MINNIE MAE. We must pay no attention to them now, Preacher. . . . Are they in the balloon?

PREACHER. Where else do you think they would be hollering like that from. (*He studies his watch.*)

MINNIE MAE (*sleepily*). My little girl. She's lost her cherry so many times. I used to think that was a very coarse expression when I lived on earth. Nothing seems coarse to me now.

PREACHER. You have tasted of the waters of Lethe, my darling. It's by far the finest water.

MINNIE MAE. Well, it's an unbeatable draught, whatever else it is.

LADY TUTTLE (*screams from the balloon*). I have been scalped alive! I've ruined my petticoat and gown, my sheer stockings, my teddy bear. Everything is a mess of . . . gore. (*She faints in the arms of Antelope.*)

MINNIE MAE. A cold wind is blowing from the north-northeast.

PREACHER. We must go right down.

MINNIE MAE. Wait for the balloon to go, as the instructions say. (*The balloon begins to ascend slowly with the married couple inside.*) I'll see you next year, again, angel! Have a good trip, a good good trip. Avoid air pockets! Don't lean overboard. If you begin to drop, throw out any heavy trunks, etc.

PREACHER (*singing as he watches the balloon rise*).
　Gosh all get-out golly gee,
　faster riding, dear Jehu flying,
　horses and clouds and dying winds,
　Oh gosh all get-out golly gee.

MINNIE MAE. Are we alone at last, Preacher?

PREACHER. Alone, alone. (*He kisses her, begins to make love to her sleepily.*)

MINNIE MAE. To those dark forgetful waters! To the black current. . . . Oh, Preacher, there is only one thing that haunts us all, the great great embrace, deeper than all the graves, the great thrust, the cry clear from the beyond, repeated again and again and forever again.

FROM THE TAROT
OF CORNELIUS AGRIPPA

FREDERICK MORGAN

In the early **MORNING** a small boy leaves the house where he has lived all his life with the old wrinkled woman who may be his grandmother. The kitchen, through which he tiptoes, holds a murky, peppery smell—but outside, the dawn air is fresh and a little chilly. Smoke rises from the chimneys of the houses down the lane; in one of the yards a dog barks. The boy has wrapped bread, cheese and a few apples in a large red handkerchief tied to the end of a stick which he carries over his shoulder. The back door creaks; he hears a moan, and choking cry, from deep within the house; but he does not look back. He will never return. —And now, in yellower light, the cocks begin their crowing.

At the **WORLD'S END** is a small hut in which each of us will undergo the final interrogation. It stands in a clearing, on top of a low stony hill at the center of a scrubby jungle filled with ruins. You will arrive at that place late on a gray afternoon, when no man, beast or bird is stirring. You must stoop and crouch to enter the low doorway. Inside, a great hand seizes you and forces you strongly down to the floor of damp earth. Looking up through shadows, you see at last your ancient judge: a huge man—hairy, naked, powerful. He stands reticent and still, without heaviness, his arms at his sides. His head may be that of a bear, an owl, a cobra. His eyes burn; he is content with nothing but the truth. As he questions you, the walls of the hut disappear, and you are alone with him at the center of an enormous darkness, from which you are watched by billions of eyes.

In a farmhouse in an out-of-the-way valley lives a **MAGICIAN** who can take any shape he pleases. As bull he mounts his fleshy cows, as trout he glides in the bordering stream, as hawk he circles high keeping watch over his domain. When travelers come to the door, he may as ogre send them screaming—or, in the form of a cheerful farm wife, welcome them to the hearth and a hearty meal. Intent on learning his secret, a boy came to the house long ago to be his servant and apprentice. He sleeps in an attic room, and at first glow of dawn peers out from the small window over quiet fields, in hope of a revelation. But after twenty years he still does not know his master's true form.

During the last ages of an ancient planet the inhabitants withdrew more and more deeply into its core. Content with a darkness in which many gems glowed, they returned to the surface only rarely, to re-envision the stars. These beings were kin to mineral and had no distinct notion of death—for each in a manner lived in each and all shared in the conscious existence of that world. The dying of one was the coming-to-life of another; the life of each was participant in the knowledge of all. And even as the race itself moved imperceptibly toward extinction, it became aware of its own rebirth, as in a remote mirror, in another dimension of the universe.

One being, however, detached himself from that communion and flew alone, his mind clenched and acute, into the stars. Inured to time and distance, he held within him the beginnings of an individual history. After an almost infinite voyage he reached our earth and took shape as a **MAN:** small, with dark skin and dark blue eyes. For many years, it is said, he lived in one of our great cities, endlessly walking the streets, staring into shop windows, speaking but seldom. One winter morning his body was found lying on the pavement, a frozen crystal . . . It is not known how well he understood our ways, or what he was thinking of when he died.

The **TRAVELER,** in sandals and lionskin, treads the hot stones of a desert extending far into time. He breathes earnestly and steadily, his eyes locked in a forward gaze. For no reason at all he has confidence in the existence—parallel to the desert—of a vast, leafy forest under whose branches he will some day withdraw and come to rest. But he sees no immediate necessity for this decision and indeed rather enjoys the strong ache of his skin charring in the remitless sun, of his feet hardening to clubs by impact with the rocks. Restless and determined, he strides forward with a vengeance.

Although he has no way of knowing it, such a forest in fact has its being, and is at hand—invisible to him. And he himself is visible at every moment from within its borders. Animals live there, whose textures blend with the inward patterns of light and shade. Couched in coolness, they watch from golden eyes the traveler passing along the naked waste. Will he walk for ever?

A man robed in blue and a woman robed in red were walking to the end of a vast rocky plateau. The dry air smelled of chicory; an endless unappeasable wind was blowing. Behind them, in a small stone house at the center of the plain, an old man robed in black waited silently . . . The man and woman reached the edge, looked down: their unified vision penetrated the mists rising from a damp, torrid continent extending itself like a wet animal many miles below. Dense fiber of jungle, layer upon layer of living matter, network of forms in growth and change, intricate spawnings. Foretaste of interdependent entities in infinite multiplications . . . Two pairs of eyes co-ordinated their observations, two minds calculated the forthcoming unravelings, a statistical determinism was established, a myth and a history projected one million years into the **FUTURE.** The two beings (and the third) retired then to their own austerity, retaining in their thought the sparse erosions of the sand and the scent of chicory. —This event occurred on a planet so far away that its light has not yet come to us.

In the city of the **SUN,** the people wore white robes by day; at night they slept a sleep without dreams. Observing ceremony in all their associations, they never raised their voices: hatred and jealousy were unknown to them. Indeed, they enjoyed an almost un-interrupted happiness. Men and women ate in privacy, but made love in the open—under the tropic foliage of the vast green parks. Couples remained together only for a day and a night, and new combinations were continually being formed. The children were raised in common. Each month, on the night of full moon, an infant girl and boy were sacrificed to the Moon and Sun, and the great chalice containing the redemptive blood was passed from mouth to mouth. Visitors from foreign lands were welcomed courteously as guests, but after three days sent on their way again under pain of death. At the center of the city gleamed the Library of white marble wherein the annals of the race are still preserved: here, before retiring to the final quiet, each citizen deposited the book of his own life.

The **ANIMALS** could not understand what love was. A man who was their friend tried to explain it but found himself running out of words. "When you love," he brought out at last, "you know that existence has meaning and that you yourself are a part of that meaning." The animals looked at one another in silence. Then an elephant made reply: "This feeling you have expressed is something we animals are continuously aware of from the very fact of being alive. It would appear that you men begin at somewhat of a disadvantage, and can only under special circumstances come to know life in its fullness."

One midsummer day a **WOMAN** wandered alone into the forest which had been for centuries the undisturbed kingdom of the animals. Having walked for hours and lost her way, she was all at once aware of her weakness: breathing deeply, she sank to the ground. Great trees rose up on all sides, through whose high inter-mixed branches the failing light filtered down. Soon she was asleep; and while she slept the animals came to look at her. They discussed among themselves what should be done. Some held that she should be put to death, others were in favor of carrying her beyond the border of the forest and forbidding her ever to re-enter it. But the elephant, who was the eldest among them, stood for a long time in silence looking down at her. "She will stay," he said at last, "because this is her home which she has chosen." The other animals were content and went on with their business. And a lynx came, and nestled against her shoulder, and a tiny green serpent began to coil himself about her ankle.

When I emerged from the last and greatest *UNIVERSE,* I found myself on the shore of a small lake surrounded by trees. A wind moved quietly through the branches and touched my face. A late light glowed in an evening sky behind which I knew there was no other. I stood; the trees swayed softly; water-sounds urged themselves coolly over the threshold of silence. Before me a woman lay in the grass, which was dotted here and there with dark blue blossoms: she was frail, human, naked. As I approached her, she smiled and slowly opened herself to me, holding apart with her hands the duskily tufted lips of her sex. Her voice spoke, "Take and eat"; kneeling, I tasted her; thousands of wings rose, beating, from the margins of the lake. Then, as she held me strongly, I released myself in her as into an ocean. For a moment of birds— that hovered, descended—we were one being: but in the minglings of our aftersleep, and even as I grasped again at her glowing shadow, she grew beyond me into the fullness of her ancient sovereignty. I found myself at large in the immensity of her womb, seeded with the imminence of stars . . . And so it was that once again I descended the ladder of being.

FOUR PIECES

FAYE SOBKOWSKY

I

*Where are the children left in this world who
do not raise their fists to their parents?*

Father I was not allowed to mourn you, mother would not let me,
but only allowed herself to grieve for you.

I am a quiet little man, I don't bother anyone. I have a tiny
shadow, my pish hardly makes a splash in the toilet. How can I
tell you of my fears? How I play dead every night in my life? And
how finally I must leave my apartment tonight to say the formal
prayers?

Father I was not allowed to mourn you, I was not allowed to
dream of your death, but let me dream of you Norman. I feel your
death. Your face was as wide as a wheatfield, broad as a plain.
My life lies before me like a plain with its burnt wheatfields, and
father you are pulling the plows with your great arms. Norman you
were meant to ride in glittering carriages through the lands to show
that you too were a man. Norman with his arms full of needle
marks. Norman's mother brought him to a public clinic so doctors
could drug him and finally glut his body with poisons. Father's
powerful body became soft soft and yellow, but Norman never knew
such a body. He carried his flesh in bags, his mother had sewn a
special pocket for his pisher. His arms pinched with needle marks
and soft yellow scars.

Norman stood in the hallway, though his mother tried to keep him behind doors. But Norman would not let himself be locked up, baby tears from this grown man. Norman did not know how to talk but brayed so loud that my fingers trembled around the handle of my teacup. He brayed so loud that I could not escape his voice, that it became locked in my memory. As did father's words, father who knew how to talk but stopped by himself.

Bray Norman, don't hide the braying. Father could not even do this, he only opened his doubled fists. And now I am hidden in this apartment afraid to move. What does it finally mean to have such a father?

We left father behind for two days in the old apartment, mother and I, while we set up the new one. We did not want him to hinder our moving. Also mother wanted to scare him, to show him that she could leave him. And he afraid that he was really forsaken did not move from the apartment, did not move from the spot. And when we came back father did not greet us with hate but tried to help us gather the few broken pieces that littered the ruined apartment, with its holes and its mice and its stained mattresses.

I walk out of the apartment carrying the velvet sack which holds my prayer shawl and phylacteries. The neighbors are quiet, the hallways are quiet, Norman's door is locked. Norman's mother is walking along the avenue. Her head is covered with a shawl. She cries to passers-by, I gave birth to a son for you and see what I have done for you, I have killed my son for you. And the avenue stretches out before me, its stray grasses scent the air. I press my body lightly against the walls of the apartment houses and use them to guide me.

II

Rosa is buried at the edges of Madja, buried in the days, crazy in the night and she is filled with Madja. Madja at the edge of the earth in the frozen places. Madja where your eyes can rest when you come with your horses. God if you would have allowed her tongue to curl out like a lovely flower, to grow a length so that she could swallow it over and over.

Orange trees across the plain, and the plain was open and grey. There were a thousand soldiers moving across the river that cut the plain. Shasta on the plain with rocks in his boots. These rocks were from the mountains he had crossed. It was Shasta who screamed God pity us as his soldiers moved through the wastes of the mountains. On the glacial divide hundreds of orange butterflies had surrounded them. Through the mountains with Shasta wanting God's pity and the men with the carcasses of smashed butterflies on their arms. And then they saw Madja, the plains with their orchards, with their aqueducts, with Rosa and the swinging hips. But Rosa was already hidden within the weeds of the river so that they thought they saw the shape of a woman but it was ha, ha the land turning dark and she safe within the weeds of the river as the soldiers lay that first night home without fires because there was no wood except the wood of the thin orange trees away and around which the boys of the state stood.

Then the day broke and Shasta met Rosa but she turned away from him when she heard the bells signaling the midday meal for the children who watered the orchards. Thousands of them were lined up and driven in trucks to the kitchens. The horses and the trucks moved side by side. In the trucks smooth hairless young boys with the scent of oranges coming from their skins. Rosa, Shasta said as she moved from him, I will make your belly as wide as fifty trees shooting up from the earth. I will change you until your eyes are empty and you will be ill for the rest of the days of your life.

The trees were pegs along the river. Rosa and Shasta moved into the mountains. Rosa with the short skirts and the flat bosom which excited him more than the busts of women with fat nipples. But she locked within the world of a child knowing that she shall always be abused until one day she shall lie red in her blood and her body finally and completely empty. And now there were others who dreamed of her. His soldiers who used the whips from their horses on men and who broke women inside with their shafts that they thrust past the place that could hold them, past the meat and into the body itself.

Come Shasta said and his voice was quiet as he fingered his cross. Let the houses sink in Madja and the orchards that surround them, hiding the children. Shasta will nurse Rosa with his male parts though it had been Shasta who had come upon her many years ago by the river. The boy with the thin hair barely wrapping the chin, beneath his underwear half-erect the little head pushing weakly to smell the dead air. Shasta whose horsemen can be seen riding across the plain with light sacks of extra children. Shasta digging his boots into the flanks of his thin seamed horse, screaming among his men.

He sits beside Rosa, but Rosa is finally sleeping. She fills his shack with her body. Bells and the few warm senseless days of her childhood and sabbath candles warm her dreams. The trucks, Shasta with his God and his many genitals are finally useless to her.

III

Mother wanted me to write a letter to the Restitution Office. She wanted me to say dear sirs: this is the daughter of R—— T——. Our mother is sick, our father just died. We would like to know if you are taking care of our father's case since she can not come up herself. I did not want to write this for her. I knew the case was closed, that the Germans had set a date many years ago when all claims for restitution could be made, but still she insisted.

This is a simple story. It is the story of a family that finally could not exist, though mother had once said a family is the most important thing in this world. "When we are together my children no one can hurt us. There are no wounds so bloody that I can't bind them, no pain so strong that I can't comfort." Ah, but what a family mother herself came from. A house full of children using their strength to beat each other. There was hate in the air, spilled blood, half-grown fists. Her sisters with erect little breasts, and bits of hair under their arms.

When a man becomes insane for what ever reason he should be killed immediately. There should be special executioners for this job. At first the family will cry, but later it will be better this way. Just the same for crippled children, blind men, and the entire human race. The earth should become one charnel house and the flesh of all families should melt. As father changed, as father's world filled with monsters and memories of children he had once killed so ours changed. In Auschwitz he had loaded trucks of naked little boys and drove them to their death.

Let me be the last to survive in my family. I will not spare myself. I will bury my brothers and sisters side by side or rather let mother be in the middle and the children on either side. I will look for the cemetery where father is lying dead, then I will haul their bodies and place them near father. And then I will make a place for myself. I write the note. But mother can not decide whether finally she wants to make the claim. This is as it has always been. She will not make the admission. She will not say that she married such a man.

She calls the Restitution Office from a pay telephone. She leaves the receiver smelling from spit, a sucking candy in her lips. She cries I will be faithful to the memory of my dead husband. When we are in school she does not call the Restitution Office, she calls the police. Her fingers tremble while she dials operator, "Any accident? No small boy run over by a car? No pretty little girl raped?"

The avenue is grey and there are wings of insects between the cracks. After school mother takes us home. The house is filled with the smell of moth balls. Mother cuts her fingers on coat hems. There are strange men's pants lying on the sewing machine and the bobbins are lined up in a row.

IV

1

I have begun bleeding. Mother takes an old pillowcase and folds the cloth several times. She gives this to me and checks my flow by making me pull down my underpants. Then mother forgets. The cloth becomes blood-soaked, it sticks to the wool hairs. I am afraid to go near father, that he will notice the new smell. I am afraid to bend because the cloth is not pinned properly and bulges when I bend. I am ashamed to go to the drugstore. I want to take a bath but there is no hot water. I will have to wait for the weekly bath when mother heats pails of water and drags them down the hall.

For the school outing I place another cloth over the one I am wearing, afraid to tear it from my body. I run down the streets with the ocean breeze coming from one direction. But the smell is not fresh, there are splintered claws covered with oil and soft jellied bodies leaking fluid.

I sit in front of the bus, next to a cross-eyed girl whose mouth smells like blood, while the other children laugh and play their transistor radios. Finally the class is walking on red cobblestone. I am left at the end of the line. The teacher screams, hurry, hurry or I will be left behind. At lunch time I wait until the other girls leave the bathroom. Then I lock myself in behind a stall. I begin crying, softly, I always begin this way, first softly. Then I separate the hairs with toilet paper that I have soaked in the luke-warm water of the public sink. Soon the bus will move again and the ocean breeze will fill my thin hair. I will run through the streets so fast that my sticky thighs will not bind me, to mother who is leaning against the kitchen wall, her face buried in the wall with her headaches. And to father who is lying on his cot with open eyes.

2

Fish cakes, lemons cut in four, and my father with cut fingers. Everyday he fishes off the pier in Coney Island and brings home fish in buckets. Mother spends her winter days with the Polar Bear Club. She keeps the knishes and coffee hot. The white socks mother wears form bagels round her legs. Sometimes mother will cook the fish for the members of the club. I do not grudge these to Fanny, Marilla, Booker T. Washington and the last Mohican since we are all pure and do not disfigure each other. We are apart from big City hospitals, we must guard our health carefully and try to prevent wounds.

Fix me so that I'm fixed. Alter me I say to Marilla. Don't let me enter into the world able to bear children. Have pity on me Marilla. Marilla punched me and for several days I could not move but then my insides changed. I took a job in the five and dime store because I loved my mother and father and wanted to help them. I was able to buy bloomers for my mother at cut-rate prices. I was able to buy towels for the club. But I felt safe in this world because inside I knew I was dead. There will be no babies from my body.

And on those fine evenings when I stand on the pier and watch father fish, I let my blouse fill with the wind.

TENDRIL IN THE MESH

WILLIAM EVERSON

To Susanna

PROLOGUE

So the sea stands up to the shore, banging his chains,
Like a criminal beating his head on the slats of his cage,
Morosely shucking the onerous staves of his rage. And his custom
Of eying his plight, with malevolent fondness, never is done.
For he waits out the span of his sentence, but is undismayed;
He stands and expects, he attends
The rising up, the crest, the eventual slump of the sun.

For he bears in his groin his most precious jewel, the sacred
     fire of his crime,
Who pursued, like the beam of a laser, its solemn command,
Across the shires, red charts of his soul, the wrinkled map
     of his hand. And his heart,
Ridiculous, by someone denied, of a country preferment,
     never quits,
But clutches its need, like a duck. Somewhere his stain
Discolors the bride of defilement, whom rapine requested,
     under the form of his need, a ventral
Oath. But parched without peace, a swollen defeat, the
     cunning sleep of the slain.

Pluto, regnant occultist, lord of the lorns of lost space, the
      serene distances fringing the skirts of the night,
Gleaming back from his visor the farthest, most tentative
      beam of the light,
Whom Kore constrained, with her hesitant breast, above his
      drooping narcissist plant,
To twine in her arms his loud male thong, his truncheon
      desire, and the flex and thrill of his chant.

She was bud. Daughter of Zeus, the Father, whose need Pluto was,
Of the incestuous darkness the daughter provokes in the sire,
When she comes of the blood; when a menstrual spurt, astart,
      pulses out of her loin,
And she quivers her sleeks, and exclaims, and her mother
Nods and denies, and watches her wander, bait for the god,
Believing it well; though she frowns, she smiles and sighs.

So pitiful Pluto, occultist betrayed, by the quince
Of a maid ensorcelled, daughter of god, of himself unable,
      succumbed and was drawn,
From the cool of monastic deeps, the slats of his cage, where
      he beat his brains,
Where he knelt in prayer, and shook the chains of his vows,
And clawed his breast in a rage. Persephone smiles,
The pomegranate seed in her pouch, her jewel of rape, and
      the stain
Of his lust on her lip. She measures his term. Cringing,
He sleeps on unappeased, in the hush of the solemnly slain.

Now sign the plight of all sires, who groan in their sleep,
When their daughter, divested, glides by in a dream,
Alight with a mauve desire, as of spring,
When barley is born to the year. O sing
Of all sires, whose passion, Plutonic, gnarls in the heart
In the immemorial fashion
Of fathers, and groan of the unspeakable thing.

But fight through to the forcing. And, gasping, pull back to see
In the dream if the hymen is crisped on the violent cod like
     a ring
Of her lips, torn flower, salt clung
Spoil of her triumph. But the aghast heart
Foretells in terror the shrink, the shy inexorable cower
Of the repulsed flesh. But an increase of need.
Oh my God the terrible torch of her power!

I

And it creams: from under her elbow a suffix of light, a sheen
     of kept being,
What the gleam from along her arm prefigures of quest.
I sense over slopes a rondure of presence invoked.
In the small of the girl, where hips greet the waist,
A redolence lurks in the crease, a rift of repose.

And I take in a long loop of arm everything seascapes
     prefigure of dusk:
Sycamore-sweeps, the tableaux of massed chaparral, a rouse
     of rowans.
Let sea-licked winds wrap the inch of their roots with evening
There to compose what the chewn leaves of the tan oak
     pucker up on the tongue;
And there, like a wand, wonderment's long awakening,
     strong shaftings of light.

No, never. Not one shall survive. When two such as we are
     outlaunched on desire, neither one comes back.
We have staked out our bodies on mesas of glimmering vetch.
We have mapped territorial claims on plateaus ripe for inclusion.
Sentinels spring up alarmed: the guardians of places remote
     are alerted to cover our foray.

Scalptakers, yes. And have waited out eons of stealth to stalk
     our quarry.
Now our needs converge; we join in a scuffle of perns.
The nets and the spears of beaters off there in the dark
     enflank us.

When the cry of the hunter broke over the flesh we fled them afar.
We enmeshed our bodies in the thickets, entoiled in the brush.

I am old as the prairies and wise as the seams of worn granite,
    but she is new burgeoned.
New as the minted tin, as sleek as the calmness of ivory
    engravers have tooled for emblems.
A girl like the glide of an eel, like the flex of a
    serpent startled.
But I catch her in throes of pulsation; we are wantoned in groves.

Crotch and thigh; she is reft. Let me break white flesh
    asunder to cock this woman.
In the glimmer of night a wedge of fern configures her croft.
Maidenhair snuggles the cleft. Its shadow conceals and defines.
When I dip my lips to drink of that spring I throat the torrent
    of life.

For passion subsumes: what is focused is fixed, denotes its
    spang of vector.
A long supple swell of belly prescinds from extinction.
When I reach above for the breasts my arm is a laser unleashed.
I have knifed through dooms that spelt long since the death
    of man's spirit.

I have fastened my heart on the stitch of your voice, little
    wince of delight in the thicket,
Where the slim trout flick like a glint of tin in the
    pesky shallows.
Salacity keels; our itch of an ardent desire consumes and
    engorges my being.
I cannot look on your face; but my fingers start toward pockets
    of peace that lurk in your armpits.

Wild stallions of shuddering need squeal jumps of joy at
    your whistle.
I feel them snort in my ribs, they snuff for foods long bilked
    in their pleas for existence.
Now they snook and are all transfigured in sudden
    aerial manœuvres.
They skip like gnats in the shafts, made mad of your moan.

Give me your nipples to lip and your ribs to caress,
Take down from your shoulders the silks that have baffled the sun.
But retain as your own the cordage of menacing loves,
Those fingers of others before me that seethed and passioned,
Those hungers you held in the crimp of your flesh,
    confounding possession.

For I sense the pungence of death alert in your loins,
    little woman:
All men in the past who have lain on the wand of your body.
Your belly is seeded with sperm, the slick of lovers cinctures
    your waist like the wake of snails.
I cannot expunge from your flesh what they wrought, or annul
    their passion.

But do not withhold from my gaze what from everyone else
    you concealed:
The remotest part of your heart that you kept immured like
    a jewel.
When I touch it to see in your eyes the sheerest expansion
    of terror,
To taste on your stretched out tongue as you die the tensile
    nerve of its anguish,
I know I have fastened the nail, I have quicked your core
    of existence.

For I am the actual. Telluric forces are groined in my being.
Uranian urgencies coil of their strengths in my soul's
    narrow passes.
Out of my sinews the deep starts of hunger yield
    mixed epiphanies:
The snake that sleeps in the stones and comes forth out
    of winter;
The great cat of the mountain that stalks for fawns in the
    darkening barrows.

I am the grizzly that grapples his mate in his hug of
    sheerest survival,
The salmon that jells his milt on the clutch his woman has sown
    in the gravel.
I am the river that breaks its back and pitches into the bay,
The osprey that jackknifes sidewise in surf to talon his quarry.

And I am the sea, its music, its instinct and whisper.
I encurl your rocks with my spill and embrace your shoulders.
In my estuary arms I entwine and enfold your thighs, I sleek
      your buttocks.
On my girth you toss like a chip to the crest of crude torrents.
When the great ships put out of port across my presence
Their seahorns chant me, sing mournful tones of presaging loss.

No ridge but the bone crest of power in the continent's nape.
A glaze of light is riddling the sheen of the wheat of Tehema.
Have the winds of Point Reyes, festooned with spindrift, declared
      anything other?
Do they glare for the spoil of the sun? Do they ache for the
      couches of night?

No bridge avails but the stretched out flesh of its
      coupling hunger.
Between the split of your thighs I plant spurts of
     voracious pleasure.
Not a hair of the nock that a woman widens anent the cob resists
      of a love.
On the nodes of transparent worlds we collapse, we pant
     and expire.

In all darks is my joy defined, that plaza, those nubian porches,
There my whole tongue turns in the col of your beating body.
In my hands of a man the sense is awake to mould idols of flesh
      for victims.
Plunged to the wrists I feel passion spurt through the instincts
      meshed in your nerves,
The peaks of clitoral quickness jetting spunk in a viscid issue.

You come back to be coaxed: I have caught you between the cheeks
      and will never be stinted.
Entwined in your thirst I tangle hair, the riatas of your desire.
In order to crest I snake angles of coupled completeness.
A flinch of fire, something struck from the meshes of passion,
      clusters my neck.

Do not think to be stronger than death; to die is to drink desire.
To die is to take at the pitch of madness one fabled stroke
    of disinterest.
I have felt on those fields the light that a passion decreed,
    spined on sheer splendor.
When you moan and expire shrewd arrows of truth, shot through
    shields of zinc, pierce my belly.

Now I ken where suns have gone down when they quitted
    our country.
It is not as if they had nothing to gain in defaulting.
Rather with us for cause they seek stratas, new zones
    of extinction.
They annihilate zeros, total steeps to expunge; like us, they
    erase their condition.

Now my fingers conclude. They have founded whole sweeps
    of existence,
Have soaked up splendor in jets, have fed to the final.
No trace remains of what was; across the line of my life
Your breast pounds and proves; the sound of your heart extols its
    ancient surrender.

II

Man of God. Tall man, man of oath. Mad man of ignorant causes.
Like the mast of a ship, like the weathered spar of a schooner.
Long shank of a man, whose hair is all whetted with frost, and
    a nick of silver.
What inch of enactment cinctured your loins and is freed?
I can feel in my knees the scruff of time's thrust as you take me.

Finger of God! A stipple of terror shudders my skin when you
    touch me!
Who are you? In your eyes is the passion of John the Baptist
    and the folly of Christ!
Do not drop me! I have never been known of man, really, before
    you possessed me!
By all men, of any, who have bruised and straightened my body,
The marks of their hands are erased of your lips. I never
    knew them!

Now teach me your deeps! Prophet and utterer of godly
      imponderable oaths, great prayers of anguish.
Guru of my bed, who have taught me koans of revealment.
Adept of niches and slots, my woman's being convulses in truth
      for your entry!
When your hands work marvels I fear I will die, will faint in
      your swells of compression.

Let rivers that run to the sea be my attestation.
You took me on Tamalpais, in the leaf, under Steep
      Ravine redwoods.
The bark of trees was broken to tear and divest me.
On the brow of the hill that brinks its base you thrusted me up
      to your God.

Beast and Christian! What manner of dog do you worship for
      Christ that you must rend and devour!
I have felt in my womb the index of Him you call God.
Do you wasten life that my flesh and my bone should be wholly
      consumed of your spirit?
What is His face if the eyes you blaze are the tusks
      of carnivores?

I have no defences against your truth and desire none.
Make me a Christian, then do what you want with this dross,
For a strange pale fury that cannot be natural consumes me.
I blink back tears of relief to feel in your hands the awe of
      Him you adore.
Is your vow of a monk meant to serve for the seal of your lust?

For your lust of a monk is a hunger of all God's seekers.
In my nerve's raw marrow I feel Him teach me His witness.
Let me go! But do not desert what you chose to instruct.
If I cannot reckon what unstrings my knees what worth
      is survival?

Let me go! No, but breach my belly with godly
      unspeakable anguish!
This split of thighs you desire is more than my means.
Your face is flensed with an awesome devouring passion.
In the flukes of contortion I fear what I see as I need it.
My body is written with poems your fingers enscrolled on
      my flesh.

Let no woman survive me, old man, mad man of the mountain,
Wily old buck of the benches and bull elk of somnolent mesas.
Monk of the seashore and friar of granite enclosures,
The mad holy man who spread my legs for entry.
As the crotch of cloistered enclosures my flesh is empaled on
    your spirit!

III

And the storm swings in from the sea with a smashing of floats.
There are hulks on the rocks where wrecks broke splintering up
    under waves.
A kindling-making wind is tearing out scrub on the jaw of
    the hill,
And the encompassed bay where fishermen loafed is found a
    cauldron of spume.

Let it blow! Now a wild rejoicing of heart springs up in answer!
After summer's stultification what more can penetrate deadness?
The nerves that have slept for so long in the simmering flesh,
    complacent with languor,
Awaken to swing their stutter of fright at the crash of billows.

And those casual loves are swept out. Only a troth as stark as
    the tooth,
Elemental and sheer as the hurricane's whetstone incisor;
Only a love as crunched as the jaw of the cougar,
When the passion-responders grope for each other under the pelt
    of the storm.

They will find in the rain what can match the spatter of hail
    on a house.
They will know where to slake when the trees break free of what
    heaps at their knees.

And they moan. Couched on beach-grass under shelter of drift
They hug each other. They watch with the zeal of love the
    hurricane's howl.

With one eye bent to the weather they see the light on the head
    at Point Reyes
Hum like an axehead held to the stone, the sparks a spurt
    shooting leeward.

Now crawl to me shivering with love and dripping with rain,
Crawl into my arms and smother my mouth with wet kisses.
Like a little green frog slit the cleft of your thighs athwart me.
The rain on your face is the seed of the stallion strewn as it
    spits blue fire.

For the lightning forks like one naked the seething thud of
    the sea.
And swells like a woman's in birth when she heaves up her belly.
She has braced her heels on the land; her beaches are benched to
    that passion,
And her crotch is the hollow, sunk low under wind-heap waves,
    when its back breaks over.

She is fouled of bad weather but never of love, this woman.
In her blood the groan and travail of a birth is being fashioned.
Her spilth like the gasp of stallions clings round her ankles.
And her vulva tilts thwart the wind's wide lip when he whistles
    his force through her body.

Now crawl to me under this driftwood hutch and cower upon me.
Warm the stitch of rain in the drench of passion and forget to
    be frightened.
But build in your womb's young realm the germ of your mother
    the sea.
For to be found in this labor sunk under a shelf she was nothing
    loath of her mating.

Oh splendor of storm and breathing! O woman! O voice of desire!
Tall power of terminal heights where the rain-whitened peaks
    glisten wet.
But the heave of slow falling sleep will follow outpouring in
    winter's wake.
This too is your meed when passion is flashed for blood in the
    typhoon's crater.

Now sleep in my arms, little newt, little mite of the water,
Little wind-beaten frog, pale delicate limper alone on
    sea-pulled pebbles.
Go to sleep and awaken in spring when your blood requickens.
And bear back to man in your flesh the subtle sign of him who
    marked you for God.

IV

Daughter of earth and child of the wave be appeased,
Who have granted fulfillment and fed the flesh in the spirit.
A murmur of memory, a feint of infrequent espousals,
And the tug of repose the heart hovers and tilts toward dawn.

Somewhere your body relinquishes creeds of defiance.
I have tasted salt salience, and savored its fragrance, have
    crested repose.
Now appeasement crouches and wends its way through my being.
I sense fulfillment not breached of strings and torches.

Kore! Daughter of dawn! Persephone! Maiden of twilight!
Sucked down into Pluto's unsearchable night for your husband.
I see you depart, bearing the pomegranate seed in your groin.
In the node of your flesh you drip my flake of bestowal.

What will you do, back on earth, when you find your mother?
Will the trace of dark lips fade out of your flesh forever?
I have knocked your instep with rapture, I have wounded
    your flank.
Like the little fish in the dredger's boat you bear the teeth of
    the gaff.

O daughter of God! When the sons of man covet your passion,
Do not forget who placed on your brow his scarab of
    sovereign possession.
In the service of holy desire bear truth for escutcheon.
And when you return to the roost of night wear the mane of
    the sun!

Epilogue

Dark God of Eros, Christ of the buried brood,
Stone-channelled beast of ecstasy and fire,
The angelic wisdom in the serpentine desire,
Fang hidden in the flesh's velvet hood
Riddling with delight its visionary good.

Dark God of Eros, Christ of the inching beam,
Groping toward midnight in a flinch of birth,
The mystic properties of womb and earth:
Conceived in semblance of a fiercer dream,
Scorning the instances of things that merely seem.

Torch of the sensual tinder, cry of mind,
A thirst for surcease and a pang of joy,
The power coiled beneath the spirit's cloy,
A current buckling through the sunken mind,
A dark descent inventive of a god gone blind.

The rash of childhood and the purl of youth
Batten on phantoms that once gulled the soul,
Nor contravened the glibness in the role.
But the goad of God pursues, the relentless tooth
Thrills through the bone the objurgation of its truth.

Often the senses trace that simmering sound,
As one, ear pressed to earth, detects the tone
Midway between a whisper and a moan,
That madness makes when its true mode is found,
And all its incremental chaos runs to ground.

Hoarse in the seam of granite groans the oak,
Cold in the vein of basalt whines the seed,
Indemnify the instinct in the need.
The force that stuttered till the stone awoke
Compounds its fluent power, shudders the sudden stroke.

Dark Eros of the soul, Christ of the startled flesh,
Drill through my veins and strengthen me to feed
On the red rapture of thy tongueless need.
Evince in me the tendril in the mesh,
The faultless nerve that quickens paradise afresh.

Call to me Christ, sound in my twittering blood,
Nor suffer me to scamp what I should know
Of the being's unsubduable will to grow.
Do thou invest the passion in the flood
And keep inviolate what thou created good!

GROWTH

FREDERICK BUSCH

In the waiting room of the surgical floor I stuff my pipe with cheap tobacco, stuff my head with patience, wonder what color a tumor is, and talk to myself about growth. My pipe is from Wilke's, on Madison; I bought it unstained, its darkness comes from time. The eight years I've had it, held it, squeezed at it, scraped it over my teeth in rage or delight, have turned it almost black; the oils of my body have painted the wood, and what I smoke is a souvenir, I'm drawing on—burning at—ninety-six months. I pack the pipe with square-cut tobaccos that look like mushroom ripenesses, fungus tones of brown and yellow decay. And now I'm lighting it over the charred edges of the bowl. Restless on plastic furniture, squinting through the smoke of almost four hundred weeks at the yellow light and dirty walls and silent doors that keep me from my wife whose body they are opening up right *now*, I open up, I burn at the time we have carried, packed and tight, stained to the color of us.

By the time the first match is in the filthy ash tray—candy boxes, butts and broken matchsticks: bone-mounds of foundered fathers and children and wives—I am back at twenty-two and so is Louise, and we're newly married, living in Greenwich Village on Morton Street in a large bathroom with cooking privileges. The knowledge we have of birth-control pills is limited to speculations in *The Times*, the smirks and whispers of a girl we knew in college (who slept with three starters on the basketball team, the top two English majors, the Physics Department's head psychopath and everyone on campus with a European accent), and general rumors that one doesn't have to somehow pay for sex with fear or effort or some kind of pain. We ignore the rumors, or attribute the news to nymphomania, we walk on Seventh Avenue, west to the Sanger Clinic, to make our marriage official and safe.

Louise wears her off-white tailored suit—she was married in it— and her face is very pale. I wear a sport coat and tie, and I think of buying Ramses over the drugstore counter in whispers. I think how old we're becoming, I cradle her elbow across the streets and feel us grow.

The clinic is in an old brownstone that's brightly lighted, the foyer is lined with posters about decision and self-determination and planning and how to make your life come out the way you think it should. A winding staircase to the right goes toward TESTING, and Louise whispers "Pregnancy tests—we don't go there now." She snorts as if she's told a joke, and I think of infinite rows of rabbits falling over in convulsions to announce a child is born.

We go to the left and into what was a living room long ago— birch logs stacked in a white brick fireplace, expecting no match —and Louise goes to the receptionist's window in the wall while I sit down, pick up *Look,* put it down, look at the green rug, look at Margaret Sanger's framed embattled face, look for Lou and see her go through a door, away. And this is the first time I actually notice the four women—each has sat as far away from the others as she can—who sit with their legs squeezed together, each one holding a large brown paper bag. Each takes her turn in staring—glaring— at me, and I look at *Look* again, then look at the rug, which still is green. I hear their breaths and sighs, the slippery sounds of skin against cloth, the whispers of their uniform bags. I think of the rabbits upstairs, falling over. I think of me falling over. Lou comes back, and she holds a brown paper bag. Her face is red and sweaty, and as she sits beside me on the vinyl sofa—it hisses and the ladies turn, then turn away—she whispers "My underwear."

I whisper back "What's wrong with it?"

"Bag."

"Huh?"

"My underwear—it's in the bag. They make you take your panties off."

"Oh God."

"Right."

"Everyone—"

"Right."

"Oh God."

"I think you're resented in here."

"I think maybe."

"Maybe more than maybe. You want to wait outside?"

"I can't."

"Why not?"

"I don't know. Yes I do: I'm scared to move."

"Well what should we *do?*"

"Pretend I'm your sister."

So we sit, the ladies pinging me with sniper fire from their eyes, Lou, giggling into her white gloves, neatly folded, I, still working on an understanding of the Rabbit Test, looking at *Look* ("New Condominiums: A Place in the Sun"), at Margaret Sanger, at the unlit fireplace, the still-green rug. One by one the ladies are called, and others come in to resent me. I think of the cold chairs against the naked skin and, when it is Lou's turn, I am nailed to my seat on the sofa by my infallible erection, which I cache beneath a tent of glistening condominiums. Upstairs the rabbits stagger.

And then Lou, redder, her upper lip wet, beckons from another door. I shake my head. She says—aloud!—"She wants to *see* us, honey."

The ladies look. I say "Oh." I say "Well what the hell." I casually drop my *Look* before me and scutter to the door. Before I'm quite inside the office I say "Fascinating article here, really" and then I'm inside, next to Lou, on a grey steel chair in the darkened room, and the woman with dark grey hair is saying that she can't always *do* this but we *are* so young and *just* barely married, and, well, maybe she can help us start off *right*.

She is Mrs. Nusbaum, with an office large enough for her, her desk and her walls; she has three visitors' chairs inside, wedged and screwed so that anyone sitting anyplace can bump against every-place else. She smells like strong mints and the perfume counter at Woolworth's, and her sibilant *s* sprays her breath: the closets of people long dead. The red plastic rims of her glasses are shaped like cat's eyes, and her teeth are perfect and white, her large hands luminous, lovely, strong dancing shapes in the darkened room.

She says "I've been counseling newlyweds for twenty-five years. *Really.* And I always say to them first off, what I say to those who, ah, *aren't* married: *think* of each other. Keep each other in *mind.*

"Now: Louise. How many times a week does intercourse occur?"

Lou grows larger, steamier, turns her head to me.

I say, definitively, "Eleven."

Mrs. Nusbaum says "Ah."

And Lou says "Five?"

I say "It varies. It depends."

Then there is silence, and Mrs. Nusbaum says "Perfectly *normal*, of course. All I need to know is *rough*ly what the intercourse frequency is. That's fine, it's *fine*."

Lou says "I mean, sometimes people don't do it at all for a week."

Mrs. Nusbaum says "Married how long?"

Lou says "Two weeks."

"Perfectly normal, of course. It's often that way."

I say "It all depends, doesn't it? How can you measure these things?"

Mrs. Nusbaum says "Well, I'm not."

I say "It sounded like you were."

She says "This *isn*'t part of the service, you know. I thought you *want*ed advice. Certainly, *I* don't mean to intrude."

And I, with my talent for dealing with human subtleties, tell her "Well I guess it just sounded like intending."

Her lovely hands settle onto the desk and she looks at them. Then she turns to Lou and says "Take care of each other, my dear. Just do what feels *right*. That will be all."

Lou, who is always begging to please whoever talks at her from the other side of a desk, says "We will" as if we've been blessed by a bishop. "We will. Thank you so much. Goodbye, goodbye."

And when we are outside again, walking back toward Sheridan Square, and I have caviled and groused, characterized Mrs. Nusbaum by her age and odor and diction, her office furniture, the hang of her hair, Lou says "I think she was pretty nice, Pete."

"Yeah. For a detective. For an investigator for the House Un-American Activities Committee. For the Kinsey Report."

"Scaredy-cat."

"Sure."

"Well *I* think she was trying to really *help*."

"Jesus, Lou, you're even talking like her!"

"I think she just wanted us to love each other and respect each other's body."

"How many times a week?"

"Is that fair? Is that really what she was like. You know, she wasn't telling us we didn't screw enough."

"You think I'm worried about that?"

"Are you?"

"You think that's what was wrong?"

"Well?"

"Shut up."

"You're such a big baby bear, Peter. I love you so much—let's not screw for a month and then have a marathon. I don't care."

"Shut up."

"You want to go over to Dauber and Pine and buy a book?"

"Do we—do it too little?"

"We do it just right."

"Oh shut up."

We stand in the street and everything else keeps moving. She puts her hands on my face and says "Let's go around and buy things and I love you."

I tell her "You know, I got scared. In whatshername's office."

"You got embarrassed?"

"Scared. I still am."

"Oh bear—*why?*"

I watch the streets move past: "Because it's the first time I knew you were different from me."

Another burned match in the hospital ash tray. Discreet reminders on the public-address system, hush of soft-soled shoes, claps of china from the coffee bar. The yellow light on worn vinyl. Faces of the other waiters, their clenched blankness. The fear and boredom, settled onto everything—on us, who watch for news to be born—like humid mist, like choking damp, like night.

Finding our apartment means turning onto Morton Street eight years ago from Seventh Avenue South, walking to the small space between two high narrow brownstone houses. The little wrought-iron gate opens into a long dark narrow alley, cobblestones worn smooth, which widens behind the brownstones and becomes a wiggly circle, grass and earth, flagstones, three enormous trees, a high wooden fence, and two wooden three-storey houses where Aaron Burr's servants are said to have lived (this our janitor tells us, who is five feet tall, a woman in jeans with short-cropped hair who makes big paintings and fixes our plumbing several times a month). We are in the first house, on the first floor—there's one apartment to a landing—and when the door opens in, an eighth of the apartment is obscured.

The floor planks are wide and uneven, worn to a black tone of brown. The walls and ceilings are white clean plaster, the two windows onto the flagstone and trees are small and askew. At the opposite end from the door is our vast brick fireplace, charred as the bowl of a pipe, in which we burn scraps we find in the streets and fragments of our janitor's stretchers, since in the Village twelve small logs are five dollars the bundle. The bathroom, off the kitchen, is grand and white and holds our closet and storage shelves as well as the bathtub built for two. The kitchen it is off is the corner of the room between the fireplace and bath: trough with spigots; Toledo Efficiency-Eeze composed of refrigerator box from the floor to waist-height, four burners atop it, oven box above them to the height of the head; and, from the wall near the fireplace, at right angles, creating the kitchen "wall" on the other side of which, before the fire, is our dining table and its chairs, the two bookcases, waist-high, which we've painted black and where we keep our Spam and Ann Page wax beans, our Woolworth's pots, our canisters made of coffee cans: our stores.

The bookcases come from my childhood room, the table from Lou's parents' garage; the stuffed sagging easy chair—to the right of the door, near the floor-to-ceiling bookshelves that lean out from their wall—is from Lou's first apartment in Pennsylvania, before that, from her parents' garage; the camp trunk, which serves us as coffee table, used to hold my Camp Nok-A-Mixon uniforms; the bed is Lou's cousin's, the red plaid blanket we use as its spread was laid across the foot of my bed when I was eight. The books are mostly recent, and our tins of food, the clothes in the bathroom, the diaphragm hidden in the bureau, the bureau itself—from Sears, and in the bathroom too—and the toothbrushes and soap. We are new also, and we grow in a garden of relics.

Because we're poor, I order a phone we can't afford. I tell the lady at the business office of Bell that we'll need an extralong cord, since that costs more. And so we have a twelve-foot cord, which makes it possible not only to talk on the phone while sitting in the easy chair, but also to stand at the bathroom door and talk, or at the stove, or in front of the fire. Since I'm out of work, I spend our money, and Lou comes home from teaching—pale, eyes ringed black with exhaustion, shabby in an old ugly coat she bought secondhand in college—to see me pointing proudly at the phone.

I put coffee on and demonstrate while she sits on the bed. "And you can move around while you talk, you know?"

"Gee, that's lucky."

"It's three dollars more, what the hell."

"You can put it on the floor outside the bathroom and take a bath and if you talk *loud* enough—"

"Listen, Lou. I can call up and tell them we don't want it. I don't care."

"No, sweetie, we can have it."

"Thank you."

"Well what would you like me to say?"

"How about something along the lines of why don't I get a job and *make* some money instead of spending it? How about did I look for a job today?"

"You don't look like you looked."

"I didn't even buy the papers."

"So: tomorrow."

"Stop looking so goddam brave, Lou."

She lies down on her back, still wearing the imitation tweed blue coat. She closes her eyes and I look at the phone. The coffee, of course, boils over.

I say "Death."

The tears come from under her lids like water squeezed from stony earth, reluctant. She says "I'm not crying, don't worry."

"No."

"I'm sorry."

"Will you shut up with sorry, Lou? I'm sorry."

It sounds like a cough and sneeze at once, and she rolls over, curls herself up, holds her face, and shakes. The room smells of scorched coffee, and I turn off the burner and look at my boy's-room bookcases. She says "I'm sorry" and I hiss, and she cries hard.

"Lou: we're all right. We're all right."

She says "I don't *feel* all right."

"Are you sick?"

"No. You are."

"Lou, it's only a phone. Or my temper, whatever the hell it is. Only that. Don't make a *thing* out of it."

"No," she says, "I mean I think you're sick of being married. Living like this. Taking care of—"

"Yeah. Some taking care of. Letting you work your ass off, and I make phone calls on my extralong cord."

"You'll get work. It's a hard field to get into. Something'll come —I'm really not that worried."

"A little worried?"

"No. Sometimes. A little."

"Yeah, well you shouldn't have to worry at all."

"And neither should you. I don't want you working at some lousy job just for money. Something good'll come and we have to wait. We can *wait*."

I sit on the bed and say to her back "It's hard to wait."

"It'll be harder not to."

"It's hard to be married, isn't it?"

She nods her head.

I say "It was pretty hard *not* to be married."

"I'll take this" she says.

"I think you're crazy."

"Thank you."

"Well, it's not a vacation."

"I don't think it's supposed to be."

"No."

"No," she says, "but it's all right."

"Really?"

"Yes."

"*Really?*"

Her hand is wandering, crawling, making moves. "*That's* hard" she says.

I pretend I'm looking away.

"Our very own extralong cord."

I say—always saying: always—"I don't want us evading the issue, Lou."

"This is the issue. Shut up and listen. I think *this* is what we're supposed to be learning about. Making long-distance calls."

And we sleep on top of the bed, wrapped in the old red blanket, the old blue coat, to awaken in darkness, hearing from the rooms above us the voices of men.

A deep one—it burrs in the buried wall wood—says "I don't hate him."

A higher one, carefully controlled, says "I thought you were supposed to love him."

"And what would you know about that?"

"What I see. What I hear."

"So?"

"What kind of *so* is that?"

"It means so why are you coming around? So why are you here? So what do you want?"

"What you do."

"I guess you know?"

"I guess."

"Well you don't."

"Weren't you going to show me?"

The deep one says "You know—you're so campy, it's disgusting."

"How am I supposed to be? Confident? Is that how you'd like me? Well I'm not. I'm not. I'm not. I just—"

"You just want to have an affair, you just want me in your pants, you just want a slow piece of ass, don't you bullshit me. I know what you want. And you don't know anything."

There is silence, then a scraping across the wood upstairs, then Lou sitting up and pulling the coat and blanket higher across her chest, reaching for a cigarette, her hair swinging thick across her face like a heavy curtain. She says "Are they—"

I say "Yes'm, yes they are. *Boy.* Yes they are."

The higher voice says "I can go home."

The deep one says "If you could go home, you little fag, you wouldn't have come here."

The higher one speaks and we strain away from each other, reach with our senses, but cannot hear. We stay apart.

And the deep one says "Fag, you cocksucking fag, you're such a *queer.* You know nothing. Nothing. Listen: do you know what it's like to fuck a hundred-and-eighty-five-pound-man? Do you? *I* do. Plenty. You little fag queen vamp queer fag."

The higher one mumbles, and they both move away, to the far side of the room above. In the darkness I thumb my cigarette lighter and Lou bends over like a swan, arching toward my hands, not touching. The flame jumps blue in the darkness—white walls luminescent, cold; our old-time furniture like darkened ice—and it runs up the outer layers of her hair, across her brows and forehead. She shrieks and the voices bellow upstairs, and whine. I push the blanket onto her head and rub, wrap, smother at her, shouting. The room stinks of chicken feathers, burned. I rub at her face, and the voices bellow upstairs, I push, I push at her shoulders, tear the blanket away, I rub at her flesh, crush too hard against her breasts and she cries again—pain alone? Just pleasure?—and she goes over backward and while they clatter and keen upstairs I throw myself onto her, into her, up, then I stop.

She is moving too, against me in the way that is with me, welcoming, and she still moves when I cease, then says "What? What?"

I whisper "I don't know. I got frightened. I don't know."

She says "No, come on. First-aid, baby. Yes."

I say "I'm so *self*ish."

And she stops, as I have done, and we listen to the noise along the walls and through our ceiling. She touches my leg and we lie apart, uncovered, and we wait. We do wait.

And all that day three years ago, five years married and living in darkest suburban New York, I wait. I wait at the office where I type in my steel and formica cubicle. There are four of us in the small writers' room and we all type on aged manual machines, and the bright blue carpet doesn't muffle much. It sounds like an engine room and in summer it smells the way it sounds. We each work on a counter at one end of which is a two-drawer file cabinet painted brightest of blues, and we all have blue phones, and we all have no doors, and all get paid rather little, and we're all too young to be here for life, and we're all without very much talent, and it looks as if we'll all be here for life. We type out stories about education. Sometimes we go to visit schools, and sometimes we talk to teachers, but usually we stay at Greenwich, Connecticut, a few minutes from the New York State border where Lou and I live, and we write about making children's minds get born.

There are problems. Should the act of moving kids from place to place in long orange vehicles be spelled out as *busing* or *bussing?* Are sliding room separators called *expandable* walls or *expansible* walls? Do we favor enamel sinks, which are porous and collect bacteria, and which are produced by a client who buys two ad pages every other month? Or do we lean toward stainless steel, which looks cleaner, except that scouring powder scratches it into porousness and it then collects bacteria, and which is produced by a client who buys *three* pages every other month. How do we talk about sex in the schools? And what about the public relations hack whose job is endangered by his total lack of ability and who telephones one of us once a week at least, trying to place his story about unwed mothers in the schools? What do we tell him to keep him from weeping us into embarrassment? And how could we accept and shape his story, which mentions his client's mobile health office which he thinks can be converted for gynecological programs— "Thus, the district can spread more thighs with fewer stirrups at lower cost . . ."—at least in every other paragraph. There are problems.

Such as getting through some years of days there. Such as resisting the impulse to stand at the edge of one's cubicle, cry to Bernie the writer and David the writer and our Irish managing editor, whose flunked Jesuit zealotry stalks the sins of our copy, some shrill parody of house style such as "Small caps flush left boldface Does your district have a vandalism problem question mark period paragraph The Pinwheel South Dakota School District did period paragraph And they solved it in a way that comma while it doesn't itals guarantee roman results comma might nevertheless be of help to you dash dash if you recognize these symptoms in your own bailiwick colon double space flush left boldface bullet Excessive broken windows flush left boldface bullet Greater dash than dash usual breakage flush left boldface bullet Rising frequency of custodial raids into your contingency budget period paragraph Here's what Pinwheel did comma and here's how you can steal a march on public school vandals period" and such as not staring at the salt sweat stain on Ellen's sleeveless blouse as she distributes the afternoon mail, and such as not calling home to see if Lou is back.

There are problems about the commuters at the Greenwich station—I am coming to look like them: we wear the same clothes and read the same newspapers, and I hardly can mind any more. If I had a longer ride, I would drink with them in the bar car and forget that I am forgetting that a job, we once decided, was a way of staying alive so as to live the right way, on paper, at night, exhausted or not, making words that no one could parody.

And there are problems about walking from the Harrison station over the long empty field of high yellow weed and stunning sudden flowers, through an early summer hum of insect and chirring of birds, the smell of gasoline from Harrison's streets somehow comfortable among odors of dog turd and thistle and distant cut grass —the problems of Louise, who has gone to a doctor in Rye after school, and who might now be home at half past five, and to whom I will have to say my fear.

The sixty-three Corvair is there, in front of our landlady's house, and I go in and upstairs to our apartment—the living room and bedroom and bathroom up three steps, the kitchen and my study on the lower landing. I work in the kitchen more than in the study. Louise has made coffee and I smell meat cooking and I stand at the steps which divide our apartment, setting the empty attaché case on the floor, waiting.

Louise calls from the bathroom "Hey honey? Pete? Are you here?"

"No, lady, this is the police. Your husband was raped by a secretary and abducted to Rio de Janeiro."

"Sounds good. I'm glad he's getting it *some*where."

"Hey, up yours, huh?"

"Can't take it?"

"Jesus, Lou, you ought to know."

Which of course means that no one says anything, and I leave the attaché case and go to the kitchen for beer. Lou comes in, and she looks white in her white terry-cloth bathrobe. She kisses me and drinks a swallow of beer and gives it back. She sits at the table that once was on Morton Street, and once in Lou's parents' garage. I drink some beer, and she lights a cigarette and coughs, cries out —up—"It was so bad, Pete. It was so embarrassing!"

I stay where I am and close my eyes. When I open them she is blowing her nose and smoking and watching for me to ask. I hold the brown bottle at my lips and say around it "Did he find anything? Is he any good?"

"He kept acting like it was my fault I have an ovary that hurts. He looked at my temperature charts the way I'd look at some dumb kid's test. He was dirty, his wrists looked dirty—"

"Oh for God's sake."

"Well that's the way they *looked!*"

My voice gives back a tiny echo in the bottle as I say "But did he *find* anything? I don't care, you know, if he looked like Lyndon Baines Johnson. Did he tell you what was wrong?"

"He cauterized my cervix."

I think of soldering irons on the moistened skin. I think of smoke going up and Lou all white, humbled into silence and sorry for her pain, spread before him and being dutiful, scared.

I put the bottle down on the counter beside the refrigerator and say "What does that have to do with ovaries?"

"He checked them too. He checked everything. I have to go in Monday for a barium enema." She's crying again, and I hold onto the bottle as if the room is loose.

"For ovaries?"

"For cancer of anything. I don't know. All I know is I have to go in and get raped by some nurse with an enema bag. I don't know."

"Well. You're all right. I mean, he doesn't think there's anything really *wrong*, does he?"

"I do."

"Great."

"Well I do."

"Well you don't know."

"It doesn't feel like it's right. It hurts too much on my side. When

I have my period sometimes it feels like something's bursting. So it doesn't feel right, and I think it's cancer, something awful, I wish you could have come—I'm sorry! I'm sorry, Pete. I really didn't want to say something like that because—of you—"

"What the hell is that *because of you* supposed to mean?"

"Because you couldn't come and I knew you'd feel guilty. It's your hobby, feeling guilty, and this isn't something for you to feel guilty about is what I mean."

"What you mean is because I was *scared* to come."

She walks past me to the refrigerator, gets us each a bottle of beer, then walks in her bare feet back to the table we have carried for five years in trucks, on top of cars, up stairs too narrow and down stairs too dark, and she says "That just isn't necessary."

"Hey Louise, you know why you piss me off so much?"

She smiles.

"Because you can get hysterical and then five seconds later you can *know* more than me. All the goddam time, you do that to me."

She smiles. She says "If I forgive you and you forgive me—"

"If I forgive me is the neat one, and I don't want to act like I'm singing this on TV or anything, Lou, but I spent an incredibly shitty day today because I didn't go with you. I should have gone and I don't want to discuss that any more. But I should have."

"Come with me next week."

"Okay. I think I can come."

Her expression is smooth, unseamed.

I say "I will. *I will.*"

We drink our beer and there is no mood left of anything, we are waiting for things to form in the air invisibly as if we waited for water to freeze while we watched. Lou turns off the oven, and we drink some more beer, and then, lighting a cigarette, rubbing cold water into her eyes, going back to the cigarette whose smoke wobbles up from the ash tray we bought at Pottery of All Nations, she says "He thinks it isn't my ovaries. That's why he wants me to have the barium thing. He says he *thinks* the ovary's all right. He should know: he had his arm up there to the elbow. But he doesn't think it's an ovary problem, unless it's polyps or something."

I think of great red bubbles of mucous growing against the bulbous shapes I imagine Lou to carry inside. "That's good?"

"I don't know. What it *does* mean is that maybe I can have children. He says after two years of trying, and if I'm all right—"

"It's me."

"There's a way of telling."

"Thank you. I've heard about it."

"He says we should sterilize a bottle and you should, ah—"

"Jerk off into a bottle, I believe is the terminology."

"And we take it to this clinic in White Plains, he gave me the address, and they can tell him about your motility."

"My motility."

"Honey, I didn't invent this business."

"So we can tell if it's my fault. No, I know. It's all right, we're not talking about *fault*. I know. Just motility."

Lou says "So if you want to—"

"Do I want to? Do I want to get a piece of ass off a Mason jar? Huh? Me? How often does a guy get a piece of ass that's a piece of glass? Me? *Sure* I want to. Yum."

Lou says "Well I have an idea about making it fun—"

And I walk out of the kitchen, across the dark little hall, into my study that is shaggy with books and the feathered pages of quarterlies. I say back "No fun, thank you. I don't think it's supposed to be fun. I'm going to do it because it's the thing I'm going to do. But no fun." I cannot stay with all that full and empty paper and I turn around and walk back in and stand behind her chair. I put my hands on her bony shoulders and rub at them, wondering which of the rooms has frightened me more. I say "Wait and see. All right? Let's just wait."

And in the morning I call the magazine and say I'm sick. I call the school for Lou—she fears the phone receptionist's wrath—and then we boil a Spanish olive jar; Lou stays in the bedroom, brushing at the skirt of her wedding suit, which she'll wear to the clinic, and in the kitchen I watch through steam as the long jar rises and rolls, is rolled. Lou calls from the bedroom "Do you want me to help, honey?" Then, wickedly, but also with a shame (I decide): "Are you sure you don't want me to *do* anything?"

Holding the bottle with kitchen forceps, wearing only boxer shorts so as not to stain my trouser front, I call back "Yeah. I want you to stay in there."

"Are you nervous?"

"Of course I'm nervous. What if the bottle doesn't go down?"

Which is about what happens. Beside the aqua shower curtain and amid the tangs of mildew, I sit with my shorts down like a sneaky twenty-year old boy, and try to test my motility. My erection has more to do with pudding than tissue and blood. My mouth is open, my eyes squinted shut. The forceps lie agape on the aqua bathroom rug. The bottle by now is cold.

Lou scratches at the door and I whine "Louise, get out of here?"

"I could lick it up and down."

"Lou. I can't sit here whacking off while you talk like that. It's perverted. Something."

"So let me stop talking and start sucking."

"No."

"Pete."

"No."

"Please?"

"No."

"Pete."

"No."

And of course that is the rhythm I haven't had, the *Yes* and *No* of lovemaking, of writing in a stale study, of being a husband, of staying alive, and while my wife stands outside my door imploring, I masturbate my half-dead sperms through the mouth of a sterilized jar. The fit is perfect, I hear my leather heart ticking moistly in my throat, I come like a time-bomb which someone has set. The explosion is shameful, I sweat out of wretchedness nearly as much as from effort. While I cap the jar, Louise is calling, but I've used her as much as I can. I do not listen. I stare at my shorts and my ankles and wait to subside. I am locked from her, I'm my own secret lover, I am hoping to be discovered. With my dying sperms in my hand, I wait to walk and lift the latch and be found out, forgiven.

Another match, and we are waiting. She, cold in the cold bright operating room. I, in the pale hot hospital hallway of chairs and ash trays. My pipe is hotter now, the tobacco lower in the bowl, and flimsier, nearly all ash, but still burning. They are cutting her open and taking out a nodule of crazy flesh. While she sleeps— while we are waiting—a nurse carries down a frozen slice of Louise's meat, and in a microscope some stranger we might have laughed at eight years ago on Manhattan streets will take a look. He will decide if the surgeon upstairs should sigh and call the gynecologist, waiting in the hospital somewhere else, and tell him that the one-centimeter tumor over her heart is malignant, come upstairs to assist him in a radical removal of the left breast: slicing away the little droopy gland-sack and its tender nipple, and the flesh beneath the arm and on the back where the lymph glands could be cancerous too. And then coming out to tell me. Waiting for her in the Recovery Room to awaken and reach up in pain, as if in scalding water, to see if she's still there.

This is what we've been waiting for: after eight fast years, the slowest two weeks of our lives together. Our lives. From the GYN exam to now: waiting. With more difficulty, less conversation, every day. Waiting while we eat and while we sleep. Louise, the last few days no longer waiting with me. Holding herself away as if she wrapped herself in her hands and clutched herself like a sacred fragile thing away. As if she were pregnant, we couldn't make love. Or barely touch. As if we both were waiting for birth. Which she has been—the birth of loss, of what could be delivered: her maddened tissue, new emptiness. Waiting while she listened and didn't hear, my words falling onto her as if from a distance, like fat cold separate raindrops. She, screened from any sense and emotion not her own: encysted. I, wanting to shout as if she were deaf. She, listening as if she were blinded and in a country whose language she never had known.

The high charred sides of the pipe gone cool. The tiny interior ashes, sticky with spit. Does it all come out to this? The waiting, growing, fumbling through our bodies toward ourselves? The surgeon slogging in his bright green clothes as if he waded through slush—after all that growing? all that work? that clumsiness, error and faith?—to say "Okay. Now take it easy. Listen carefully. Here's the way it is."

Frozen section of eight years together, sliced and examined, these words—memory formed as prayer—are how it was. And therefore what it is. Here is what we have grown to. Here is what we have found: the flesh tearing away, the language less than adequate, the madness of continuing. I light the pipe and suck at the stem, suck through spittle to get the smoke and fire up and watch the surgeon come. I will speak before he does. I will tell him we continue. Along the perspective-lines of the corridor, starting where the angles meet, and trudging vertically *down* to me, the surgeon comes with our future in his mouth. I huff and suck on the past. I will tell him our courage. I will speak. He says, before I see his face, "Okay. Now take it easy. Listen carefully. Here's the way it is." I listen and say nothing, I see Louise reach up to her emptiness, we always were dutiful, we always had such faith, we were only obeying orders.

A BOOK OF HISTORIES

JEROME ROTHENBERG

HISTORY ONE

His childhood ambition had been to become a saint.

Hay covered the synagogue floor. It was an old synagogue, the ark carved by an Italian master. On one of the walls hung the matzo eaten at the end of the Passover seder. A metal vase filled with sand contained the prepuces of circumcised infants.

She told him she was Lilith & that if he let her go she would teach him all her names. The names she wrote down were

LILITH	ABITR	ABITO	AMORFO
KKODS	IKPODO	AYYLO	PTROTA
ABNUKTA	STRINA	KLE	PTUZA

TLTOI-PRITSA.

He told her he was Elijah.

. . . drinking beer & munching nuts

He had also warned me to be sure that the boiled milk had formed a skin.

long hose

½ shoes

sash about the loins

skullcap beneath a velvet hat

kerchief around neck

metal-rimmed spectacles

He loved to play chess & to make up riddles. "Three entered a cave & five came out"—the answer was Lot & his daughters. Or "what is that which is produced from the ground, yet man produces it, while its food is the fruit of the ground?" "A wick." Or "who was he that was born & died not?" Answer: Elijah & the Messiah.

someone had told me that if I were to light 40 candles & recite a secret incantation he would die

HISTORY TWO

The binding prevented the child from putting its toes into its mouth; also from touching its face with its fingers which may just before have touched its crotch or its toes

old fashioned gaberdine

a velvet hat with a high crown

½ boots, pantaloons & white socks

His ritual fringes reached below his knees.

The body was washed in warm water, scented with spices, & then
a beaten egg was used as an additional cleansing agent.

Then one of the beadles would remove his boots & walk over the
tablecloth in stocking feet, pouring wine for everyone.

Ordinarily she was a quiet girl, but suddenly she would begin to
howl like a dog & to speak with a man's voice. Then she sang like
a cantor, & her voice was as powerful as the roar of a lion.

"Arise, Rabbi Chisqiah, & stand in thy place & declare the worthi-
ness of this part of the holy beard."

Rabbi Chisqiah arose, & began his speech & said, "I am my Ḻe-
loved's, & his desire is toward me."

. . . by their very exterior you could tell that these were no lovers of
water & to your distress you often knew it with your eyes closed

how in Galicia, before a child was suckled, they placed part of a
honeycomb in its cradle

The men of the congregation, having a quite different conception of the meaning of this anniversary, arrived with their pockets stuffed with thistles, which they proceeded to toss into each other's beards. When they ran out of thistles, they ripped the plaster from the walls & threw it

He had found an ancient commentary which declared that when Javan would be at war with Ishmael, the deliverance would come. And now he had heard, during a conversation in the ritual baths, that Russia & Turkey were on the point of war. Russia was of course Javan, & it had always been known that Turkey was descended from Ishmael, the son of Hagar, the handmaid of Sarah.

"It cannot be otherwise," the Rabbi muttered, & his excitement increased.

hernia

hemorrhoids

He took the torah scroll & hurled it to the ground, & then he had to fast for 40 days as a penance.

HISTORY THREE

They covered the mirrors with towels, drew the blinds, knocked over the chairs, broke the dishes, & stopped the clock. Then he put on a pair of felt slippers, to accompany the coffin.

"I eat only once a day, at four o'clock. For four years now."

. . . he burst into laughter finding that he had jewish hair, jewish eyes, a long jewish nose

an enema of lukewarm water & camomile, & sometimes added garlic

He drove off at top speed to New Court, where he arrived just before four o'clock in the afternoon. One of the porters immediately announced him to the head of the firm, whom he told that the Prime Minister wanted £4,000,000 the next day, & why. Baron Lionel picked up a muscatel grape, ate it, threw out the skin, & said deliberately:

"What is your security?"

"The British Government," replied Corry.

Cutters

Jacket Pressers

Underpressers

Skirt Pressers

Skirt Basters

Skirt Finisher

Buttonhole Makers

While in one corner some stood at prayers, in other corners Jews

ate & drank, drove bargains, argued & bought hot, peppered peas

from an old woman who kept a supply under a mass of rags.

another tradition runneth thus: whiteness in whiteness & whiteness

which includeth all other whiteness

There had been few Jews where he came from. In the course of the

centuries their outward appearance had become Europeanized &

had taken on a human look, so you might even have taken them

for Germans. Then later, strolling through Vienna's inner city, he

had suddenly encountered an apparition in a black caftan & black

hairlocks. Was this a Jew? he thought. They hadn't looked that way in Linz. He observed the man furtively & cautiously, but the longer he stared, the more his first question assumed a new form: Was this a German?

. . . an awning of white silk or satin, supported on four poles & embroidered with the words, THE VOICE OF MIRTH & THE VOICE OF JOY, THE VOICE OF THE BRIDEGROOM & THE VOICE OF THE BRIDE; also with flowers & green leaves . . .

Rabbi Schimeon began, & said: Woe unto him who extendeth his hand unto that most glorious supernal beard of the Holy Ancient One, the concealed of all.

This is the praise of that beard; the beard which is concealed & most precious in all its dispositions; the beard which neither the superiors have known; the beard which is the praise of all praise; the beard to which neither man, nor prophet, nor saint hath approached as to behold it.

The beard, whose long hairs hang down even unto the breast, white as snow; the adornment of adornments, the concealment of concealments, the truth of all truths.

. . . he was like a man who takes a ritual bath while holding an unclean reptile in his hand . . .

rice boiled in milk

HISTORY FOUR

There was the rabbi, for example, who said you mustn't urinate in the snow on the Sabbath because it resembles plowing . . .

Once, he told me, while studying the law in the Valley of Genusan, he saw a man climbing a tree. The man found a bird's nest in the tree, & taking the mother with the young ones, he still departed in peace. He saw another man who finding a bird's nest followed the Bible's command & took the young only, allowing the mother to fly away—& yet a serpent stung him as he descended & he died. "Now," he said, "where is the Bible's truth & promises? Is it not written, 'And the young thou mayest take to thyself, but the mother thou shalt surely let go, that it may be well with thee & thou mayest live many days.' Now, where is the long life to this man who followed the precept, while the one who transgressed it is unhurt?"

Their fur coats, old, & fur hats, older, made a pile on a chair. Nails on the wall were the hangers, but chairs were better. Around the talkers in the cafe were bits of lemon, crumbs of cake, wetted lumps of sugar.

The doctor said: "I was told many times about women who wake their husbands up in the middle of the night—& then all she needs to come is for her husband to move near her."

two quadrangular diapers, one warm one of flannel, the other of linen, & a quadrangular piece of waterproof oilcloth. also a pillow stuffed with feathers

When her oldest son was 2½ years old, they went to the park for a walk. She led him, holding his hand. Whenever the child saw a small or large puddle he encircled it very carefully, in order not to soil his shoes. She always paid a lot of attention to the cleanliness of her boys.

In the women's rooms, where the bride was being prepared for the ceremony, it was cool & spacious. Girls danced together, lifting up the ends of their ballooning skirts; or else they stopped & talked affectedly with the musicians, trying to make their Yiddish sound like German.

awkward in her emotion she had slipped her face under the man's beard & left it buried there . . . her hands were clasped at the small of his back. As he dared a timid caress, barely sensual, on Judith's white neck, a question crossed his mind: Does God, blessed be his name, wish the death of infants?

With a sudden gesture, partly of shyness, partly the result of long training, he covered his eyes in order not to look at a woman, stepped aside, & murmured: "Good evening."

. . . the gutters, where dead horses lay for days or until a special truck came along to haul them off . . .

They conducted the queen to Solomon, who had gone to sit in a house of glass, to receive her. The queen was deceived by an illusion. She thought the king was sitting in water, & as she stepped across to him she raised her garment to keep it dry. On her bared feet the king noticed hair, & said to her: "Thy beauty is the beauty of a woman, but thy hair is masculine; hair is an ornament to a man, but it disfigures a woman."

And the sages said: "Make for me an opening as wide as the eye of a needle, & I shall make an opening for you as wide as the door of a chamber."

. . . later he was also nicknamed the Dancer of God

HISTORY FIVE

He wore a hat in the rabbinic style, but his alpaca jacket reached only to his knees, in the German fashion.

His trousers were striped, his boots glistened.

But he also had white earlocks.

Very frequently he would purify himself in the ritual bath: he would learn by heart & repeat the fantastic names of angels: & he would often deprive himself of meals.

When he was a child he had pictured God as living in the moon. You know—he said—the face in the moon. There was a saying that God looks down from the moon, & he had pictured him that way.

The hut in which he lived was ice-cold. The windows were stopped up with cushions, & the smoke of the kitchen had blackened the walls. Wild mushrooms & toadstools sprouted on the dank, earthen floor. His second wife, a lean, haggard woman, sat on a low chair, pushing her hanging breast against a baby's mouth, & crying:

"Suck, draw, draw the life out of me!"

whenever he saw his own excreta he threw up

Moreover he spied a skull floating on the face of the water, he said to it: "For drowning others you were drowned; & in the end those who drowned you will be drowned."

The tsaddik shut himself up in his room, & it was said that the floor was covered with dust & never swept. Large mice used to run around, & old ugly grey frogs jumped in dark corners. The lonesome tsaddik treated them like well-groomed dogs. His disciples said that the frogs & mice were the souls of sinful, deceased hasidim.

Among them was one young beggar, supposedly released from an insane asylum, with a very beautiful & strong tenor voice. Whenever someone refused him charity he would intone the prayer for the dead at the top of his lungs. People stricken with awe gave him what he wanted & ran away.

"When I was born," he told George Cornwallis-West late in life, "I was so beautiful that my co-religionists took me for the Messiah. But they wouldn't think so now, would they?" he added ruefully.

Sleeping that night on the floor of a damp country synagogue, he had been awakened suddenly by a sound of distant singing. He followed it across the room to the great wooden ark of the covenant, whose doors swung open as he reached them. Inside he saw a blue light dancing before the scrolls of the law, & a woman's voice sang loudly: "I Am Afire with Love." It was the most beautiful thing he had ever seen.

not a mere fortuitous aggregation of individuals but a sacred society —a self-dedicated "kingdom of priests"

HISTORY SIX

She would drive off to the Odessa quarries, sit drinking tea with Jews at the Bear Café, buy smuggled goods on the waterfront. . . .

But the serious cafés were usually up one flight—on Division Street, Allen Street, Orchard Street, Canal Street, or on Chatham Square.

he was wearing a brown jacket, cream-colored pants, & raspberry-red shoes

Machines, needles, thread, pressing cloth, oil, sponges . . . often the workers brought their own machines, as well as the needles & thread.

When they saw her in the distance, mothers would exclaim, "The demon!" & would pull their children into the house. Under their breath they muttered: "Salt in your eyes! Pepper in your nose!"

also cafés for domino players who drank nothing alcoholic & seldom talked

Two chinamen in bowler hats, holding loaves of bread under their arms, stood on the corner of Sadoraga Street. With their frosty nails, they marked off slivers of the loaf to lure the passing Jewish prostitutes. The women passed by them in a silent procession.

There was the Odessa Café on East Broadway. . . . Others were called Krakow, Moscow, Kiev, Lublin, & Warsaw. . . .

He brought two seamen along with him—an Englishman & a Malay —& the three of them dragged a case of contraband goods from Port

Said into the yard. The case was heavy & they dropped it & out tumbled some cigars entangled in Japanese silk.

. . . the Rutgers Street Public Bath

He borrowed a comb & a necktie from an obliging detective, dusted off his shoes & faced the press, his usual, debonair self.

. . . bohemian cafés . . . noisy with dancers & accordianists

His ideals of life resolved themselves into money to spend, beautiful women to enjoy, silk underclothes, & places to go in style.

After dinner he settled in an armchair & opened a thin volume. His gangster friend had recommended *The Prince* as a way of gaining insight into the Italian mind.

"& Joseph will get a first class funeral—there'll be six horses like six lions, & two carriages for the wreaths, & the choir from the Brodsky synagogue, & Minkovsky in person will sing over your late son."

green horn

maki

griner

griner tukes

—How old were you when your mother stopped punishing you?

—When I was old enough to defend myself—then she stopped. I must have been about 16.

—Did she ever spank you?

—She *beat* me, & she threw things at me, & she hit me with sticks, & she punched me, & she pulled my hair.

With an ancient Spanish dagger—none from Sicily was available— Trafficante cut his left wrist, allowed the blood to flow, & wet his right hand in the crimson stream. Then he held up the bloody hand.

"So long as the blood flows in my body," he intoned solemnly, "do I, Santo Trafficante, swear allegiance to the will of Meyer Lansky & the organization he represents. If I violate this oath, may I burn in hell forever."

Tourine witnessed the signature with an X in ink. Sam Tucker produced a band-aid, & the two Mafia leaders hurried out.

. . . a play called *Demented America*—his final play

HISTORY SEVEN

". . . During the second week the power became so strong in me that I couldn't manage to write down all the combinations of letters which automatically spurted out of my pen. . . . When I came to the night in which this power was conferred on me, & Midnight had passed, I set out to take up the Great Name of God, consisting of 72 Names, permuting & combining it. But when I had done this for a little while, the letters took on the shape of great mountains, strong trembling seized me & I could summon no strength, my hair stood on end, & it was as if I were not in this world. Then something resembling speech came to my lips & I forced them to move. I said: 'This is indeed the spirit of wisdom.' "

a head of a carp wrapped in cabbage leaves

Sometimes it happened that during the merchant's travels in the forests a young peasant woman would wait on him, the wife of some innkeeper: she would smile up at him as she drew the long boots off his feet before he went to bed: she would beg him to raise her husband's pay. Then he did not say no: nor did he refuse to let her kiss his hand out of gratitude when he had put out the light.

. . . picking cucumbers out of a barrel of brine

If any one came within ten feet of him during prayer or before it, the rabbi would shout words like "cattle" or "robbers" & would sometimes slip off his belt & strike whoever was in his way.

. . . in the evening i brought her a white loaf as well as a dark one . . . also poppy seed rolls i baked myself . . . i thieved because of her & swiped everything i could lay my hands on . . . macaroons . . . raisins . . . almonds . . . cakes . . . i hope i may be forgiven for stealing from the saturday pots the women left to warm in the baker's oven . . . i would take out scraps of meat . . . a chunk of pudding . . . a chicken leg or head . . . a piece of tripe . . . whatever I could nip quickly . . . she ate & became fat & handsome . . .

Not only the gateway, the entire courtyard was filled with obstacles. Servant girls sang, & Reb Moishe stopped his ears, for the voice of woman leads to lewdness. The sound of gramophones came thru open windows, & sometimes a troop of magicians & acrobats gave a performance in the courtyard; a half-naked girl, wearing short breeches & a beaded jacket walked on her hands. Every step of the way was fraught with danger. Servants sat on the stairs, grating horse-radish & slicing onions. All the world's females seemed to be waylaying Reb Moishe, trying to deflect him from the narrow path of righteousness & lead him to Gehenna. But Reb Moishe carried his weapons—his walking stick. He closed his eyes & pounded the stone flags with his stick.

vodka & currant cake

Zanvl took hold of the bag; then with the swiftness of a young gypsy he lifted the door off the hinges. Warm steam beat into his face. He took out the whiskey, made the horses drunk, & put shoes on their feet. Then he led them softly out of the stable.

We used to make holes in the sand with the heels of our boots. All the holes had to be approximately the same size. Then we would all piss into these holes. The one who filled his hole first was the winner.

Every morning he went from door to door after he had prepared the synagogue. He tapped on the shutters with his wooden hammer & called out weakly: "Jews, rise! It is time to serve God."

a silken man

he had completely incarnated himself into a sacred lemon

I ENVY YOU
YOUR GREAT ADVENTURE

COLEMAN DOWELL

"Cheryl is the only gentleman in the American Theatre." Omerie said it firmly. "You should let *her* produce your play."

Augustine was thoughtful. "Naturally, I'd thought of her *first,* but one mustn't ignore completely those others." It was an entire statement and having fashioned it he turned as though to open the window and let it fly like a bird too lovely to be kept imprisoned. He stood looking down onto the formal gardens and the lemon groves beyond. In the same musing tone, he said, "There goes the Duke. It really is too bad that he looks like a gardener."

"Well, the head gardener looks like a duke, so I suppose that balances the ledger." Omerie made an Aubrey Beardsley gesture with his left hand but quickly realized that the gesture was not successful because he had no left hand. He looked intensely for a moment at the space that should have been occupied by the hand. "Augustine, wasn't it extraordinary that there was no blood when my hand fell off last night?"

Augustine smiled at him, very nicely. "Not in the least. You always were fastidious." He yawned and said, "I suppose we should do something or other about dressing if we're to go to the casino tonight."

"We would attract more attention if we didn't dress."

"Oh, who cares what they think in Estoril? The nicest thing about Portugal is that one can be oneself here, and wear dinner clothes any time."

"Do you think," said Omerie, "that we will ever go back to New York?"

"Who knows—or cares, for that matter? Perhaps we'll slip back some summer and peer in on the carnage? If we stay at the Waldorf, dine at Sardi's, and refrain from smoked glasses, nobody will know we're there."

They dressed at a leisurely pace, occasionally ringing for this or that, and after an omelet and strawberries in the garden and coffee with the Duke, they got into their automobile and drove the short distance from Setais to Estoril where they won money until Omerie's right hand dropped bloodlessly from his wrist, which meant that he could not handle the chips and so had to stop playing. Augustine stopped playing out of sympathy and boredom and cashed in their chips.

Humorously, he told Omerie, "Now I shall have to feed you like a little bird. Will that amuse you?"

"How can I tell? It might be more amusing to sip things through a straw and simply not bother with the rest. However, we shall, of course, see."

When they returned to the palace they walked for an hour in the gardens and groves, talking of this and that. A touch of mist muted the night which without it would have been like a golden trumpet. Occasionally a cock crew and the two young men agreed that the harsh note was as destructive to the night as a political discussion to a dinner party. Since they feared the false propaganda would penetrate to their rooms, they sought out the offending creature in the stables and Augustine wrung its neck with finesse so that his white gloves should not be soiled. They then returned to their suite and were ready for bed in a scant two hours. This was the moment to which they both looked forward—when, in brocade and silk, they settled comfortably into bed each night and Augustine read aloud his play. Tonight would be the four hundredth reading and the number appeared significant enough to lend an air of extra festivity to the occasion. When the tiny mother-of-pearl marijuana pipes were lit—or, tonight, only one, which Augustine from time to time held to Omerie's lips—Augustine began to read. He was in excellent voice and his rendering of the part of the Amethyst Tongue Scraper, for whom he would ask that Fontanne be engaged, was especially effective. They had heard recently that Alfred was sick, so the role of The Tongue, which had been tailored to his talents, Augustine read sadly, hauntingly, with a touch of doom that was, according to Omerie, the only way it should be read. The locale of the play was A Mouth, and the characters represented objects introduced into it over a span of twenty-four hours. It was allegorical and poignant, almost excessively the latter, so that both young men were reduced to tears when The Mouth finally closed for the last time on the horde of brightly colored Sleeping Pills. However, Augustine did not for long allow emotion to color his fanatic objectivity concerning his magnum opus. Indeed, it seemed to Omerie, who did not hesitate to say so, that the release of tears led Augustine to a harshness of judgment that verged perilously upon the *professional*. Tonight was hardly an exception. The loveliest speech in the play began "*The* full-form'd phalluscy—" which was so exact, so immediate, that Omerie's eyes produced more tears at Augustine's insistence upon changing "the" to "a."

"It *spoils* it," Omerie moaned between sips at the held marijuana pipe. " 'A' is so terribly *general*—the edge, the beautiful *hurting* edge of the specific—" He choked and motioned with his streaming eyes for Augustine to take the pipe away. Augustine was pitiless, adamant. At last Omerie, knowing the battle to be lost, told him with a touch of well-justified malice, albeit mixed with sorrow, "Very well. But you will get no star to play an 'a.' You might as well forget Marlon." This did make Augustine thoughtful, at least, which he hated, so that his "good night" was circled with coolness like drops of dew. Lying in the dark, Omerie reflected that this was far from the first time they had fought over matters aesthetic, and that he had always, heretofore, been the one to concede. *Heretofore;* tonight he would not do so, nor tomorrow, nor the day after that. He would carry his convictions like unfurled banners in his eyes, to the very edge of the abyss which is the only surviving child of battle. He fell militantly asleep and dreamt of Jeanne d'Arc.

The following morning, or noon, when they had arisen and were performing their toilettes—or rather, when Augustine was uncomplainingly tending them both—Omerie's decision of the night before to carry his banners silently in his eyes took on an unavoidable air of the prophetic, because when Augustine was scraping Omerie's tongue—their tongue scrapers were made of palest jade—the tongue came away with the scraper. Omerie marveled, of necessity, silently, and wondered if he could be just a touch clairvoyant. At first the thought was pleasing but then images of fat clairvoyants—

Madame Blavatsky, Eileen Garrett (though her eyes were splendid) and Marie Powers—took his pleasure from him and he determined that he would not be clairvoyant; not in the least.

When Augustine had scraped his own tongue, he said to Omerie, his face wearing an expression of slight displeasure, "We will really have to go straight to Italy now. I do dislike missing the Spaniards this time around, but as Portuguese and Spanish are *your* languages, we will not get far with bargaining, I fear." He made a little *moue* of distaste. "Sign language is too barbaric to consider." He sat on the bidet and turned Omerie over his lap, applying their own soft tissue gently, as to a child. "I do regret the fishers at Nazare—so fiendishly reluctant, in their leathery way, you will recall—" He stood Omerie up and smiled warmly into his eyes. "But there. You mustn't think that I blame you, my dear. Perhaps we won't find Italy too soiled this time around."

He led the way to the dressing room where he dressed them both in the softest of summer flannels, pale yellow for himself and for Omerie the beautifully elegiac lilac. This was a special concession given, Omerie knew, as compensation for his coolness of the night before. Augustine usually insisted on the more dramatic expression for himself.

When the Duke's valet had packed for them, they managed to escape without having to bid the Duke farewell, a thing they loathed doing for the Duke was old and sometimes grew slobbery and embarrassing on the subject of Perhaps Last Meetings and so on. As Augustine had said to Omerie the last time it happened that they were caught in a Farewell Scene with the Duke, "Last Time, Pastime," and Omerie had murmured admiringly.

They drove to Lisbon where they abandoned their automobile in favor of a chartered jet plane to carry them to Rome. Augustine spent some time forward with the pilot but now and again he would come back to where Omerie lay among their special cushions and feed him bits of peaches soaked in an infusion of chablis and hashish. It was typical of him, they both felt, that he could interrupt his own pleasure to perform thoughtful acts. He told Omerie that the pilot possessed in equal measure the qualities of anger and avarice, and that there might be An Incident when the plane landed, although Augustine could not promise this. The unfurled banners in Omerie's eyes seemed to snap in a sudden brisk wind. Augustine appeared to be, for a fraction of a second, disconcerted and then his face resumed its customary lack of expression. After a while he went forward again.

In Rome they found a plethora of tourists and not much else. Even the fountains were unbribable; that is, they displayed nothing for which a bribe might conceivably be offered.

The nightly reading of the play became alarmingly burdensome. Augustine changed more and more words until it seemed that he was bent upon total destruction. In three nights he recklessly changed five words and abandoned two. Carnage stretched behind him bloodily. Omerie's flags signaled with increasing franticness, to no purpose: Augustine avoided his eyes. In despairing frenzy, Omerie stamped his foot, something he would never have done ordinarily. It was, he knew, an extreme measure, but he was rewarded. Augustine could not with good grace avoid his eyes when he had picked up the leg that separated itself at the knee and slid from the silken pajamas with a reproachful little sighing sound. Augustine stood holding the leg and his eyes filled with genuine sorrow as he told Omerie:

"I know I'm being beastly, my dear, but surely you will agree that it is at least partially warranted? Something quite frightfully unexpected is happening to the climate of the world when *Rome* should appear to be sterile. *Soiled* is one thing, but *this* . . . Though it is a cliché, I would welcome even a common cold as evidence that *something* of an adverse nature could still occur."

Omerie felt his misery and considered attempting a sneeze, but he knew that Augustine would see through the ruse. Also, he knew that Augustine considered sympathy to be condescending and therefore he was careful that his expression remain noncommittal. The play was the important thing, and though Augustine was kindness itself, he could, on occasion, if goaded to it (as he had been in the past three nights), take his pound of flesh even when it hurt him to do so. Omerie felt that one more excised word would be beyond his own endurance.

Fortunately, when Augustine returned to Omerie the following night, he was able to report that circumstances had taken a turn for the better. He had struck several good bargains and there had even been a slight Incident following the execution of one in the Colosseum. Nothing spectacular, but a skirmish. He read beautifully again and, to Omerie's breathless relief, returned with teasing casualness one of the abandoned words to its rightful place. Omerie was not religious, but he approached the edge of Prayer that night with his fervent wish for a really *big* Incident for Augustine; something big enough—though he hardly dared wish for so much—to cause Augustine to change the devastating "a" back to the eloquent "the."

Omerie had never felt himself to have much will power, which was a drawback, but he hadn't, he felt, individuality enough for that. His function had always been to guard the treasure of Augustine's genius and to help feed its source. It was to this end that he had learnt the barbaric Portuguese tongue, because for Augustine to know it would have been a blight on his purity of expression, like a birthmark on clear skin. Omerie crossed his handless arms upon his body in the darkness and sighed as he felt the arms loosen at the shoulders and roll down to lie along his sides, slightly bent at the elbows, enclosing him in a set of parentheses. As he fell asleep it amused him to think that perhaps this was what was meant by the expression "self-contained." He told himself that it was a thought of absurd levity under these circumstances when so much was at stake but he did not honestly feel that his little self-amusement could affect in any important way his large wish for Augustine.

He continued to wish and though there was no way of knowing whether it was in response to his wishes that such a thing occurred, Rome improved. There was, true enough, no really big Incident, but Augustine was able to report several medium-sized ones and, on their last night together, to exhibit the evidence of an *almost* satisfying one to Omerie: the thinnest line that a knife-blade had traced around the base of his throat. This had given Augustine justification to shoot, with his exquisite little eighteenth-century pistol, the man through the shoulder. Not, alas, fatally, but it gave one reason to hope for the near future. That last night Omerie lay with eyes closed in thanksgiving as Augustine read and in the process returned the other abandoned word to its place and reinstated four of the five changed ones in their pristine offices.

Omerie lay awake to the Roman night, unable, perhaps due to hunger-induced weakness, to put off any longer the revelation that what he had told himself were wishes were in actuality prayers: real prayers to a real, existing, undoubtedly exacting God. Nor could he feel humiliated by such proof of his insignificance. His smallness of mind matched perfectly the smallness of his body, which was no more, by this time, than a torso without limbs or genitals on which his tongueless head with its flagless eyes perched with a look of impermanence. It was not quite correct to say that the eyes were flagless, but the banners had furled as wish became prayer and prayer became answer. There was little actually left to wish (or pray) for; Omerie had every reason to believe that Augustine would, of his own unflawed taste, change back the offensive "a" to the sublime "the." If wishes could be called disguised regrets, then he *did* regret his inability to communicate one last request to Augustine, much too complicated for his asking eyes to accomplish. It was possibly just as well, for it was a selfish request . . . Even as he thought it, through the open window there flew a bird of bright plumage which came to rest on Omerie's bosom. The oddity of the occurrence was that Omerie and the bird could observe each other despite the darkness of the room. The bird looked into Omerie's eyes and repeated what it saw there in an accent very like Omerie's had been. When Omerie ceased to think, for fear that the voice might wake Augustine, the bird was silent.

The following noon, as Augustine dressed, the bird spoke to him in Omerie's voice, a bit hesitantly phrasing the request, as Omerie would have done—was, Omerie supposed, actually doing. Augustine was the soul of goodness, agreeing to the letter without quibble, merely remarking, because it was a fact and should be known, that he would have to postpone, and possibly miss altogether, an arranged meeting with a promising prospect. But this would not for a moment keep him from obliging Omerie, and let no more be said. When no more was said, surprise winged across his face, or perhaps it was the shadow of the bird's wing as it fluttered to the door and sat waiting there.

Augustine carried Omerie to the Via Sistina and placed him there in the sunlight on a little canvas chair, quite near the other torso with the monkey and the tin cup that Omerie had remembered from other times and envied. The bird perched on Omerie's head, stretching its wings once as though saying good-by to flight before it settled down. Augustine looked at Omerie for signs of tears at the parting—surely there should be tears? Omerie felt it too, but none came. He wondered if the bird was crying, but he could not, of course, see. And still Augustine delayed his departure. Surely some last plea to save his great work? Omerie felt it too, but none came; the bird was silent. Augustine frowned and Omerie's heart beat thickly, telling him for his gratitude that there *was* something further he could do to feed Augustine's genius: he could lie. The bird fluttered and craned its neck and spoke clearly into the crystal air:

"I envy you your great adventure." The words, new-minted, rang like bright coins dropped into the tin cup of the blind torso with the monkey.

"*Grazie—grazie*," said the torso, smiling sightlessly about, nodding his head in all directions. "*Grazie, signore.*"

Augustine smiled a smile plural and dazzling enough for a host of seraphim. He lifted his hand as though bestowing a benediction upon all present.

"*Prego*," he said, and walked away to keep his appointment.

NINE POEMS

ANGEL GONZALEZ

Translated by Louis M. Bourne

TRANSLATOR'S NOTE: *Angel González has been one of the primary exponents of what is known in Spain as "social poetry"* (poesía social), *at its best not merely a reaction to the political circumstances that characterized post-Civil War Spain, but a serious, often ironic, moral meditation on the tragedy of a society divided against itself.*

Born in Oviedo in 1925, González grew up and studied law and education in his native town. Moving to Madrid in 1950, he switched to journalism and later became a public official. In 1972 and 1973, respectively, he gave courses on Spanish poetry at the universities of New Mexico and Utah.

His first book did not appear until 1956: Aspero mundo *("Bitter World," awarded a second place in the Premio Adonais contest). This was followed by* Sin esperanza, con convencimiento *("Without Hope, with Conviction," 1961),* Grado elemental *("Elementary Degree," Paris, 1962, awarded the Premio Antonio Machado in Collioure, France),* Palabra sobre palabra *("Word upon Word," 1965),* Tratado de urbanismo *("Treatise on City Planning," 1967),* Breves acotaciones para una biografía *("Brief Notes for a Biography," 1969) and* Procedimientos narrativos *("Narrative Techniques," 1972). His collected poems were brought out in 1968 with the title of a previous work,* Palabra sobre palabra, *and revised in 1972.*

González once remarked in an interview that his first book was born from the experience of loneliness and a vague sense of inherited failure. Later, he said, influenced by the liberal example of fellow poets Gabriel Celaya and Blas de Otero, he wrote verse on the basis of his social commitment.

His critical poetry responds to what he calls "an external stimulus and a personal obsession." He sees the poem as not only a product of the historical circumstances in which it is created, but also a necessary reaction to them. His best portraits of middle-class industrial society detail with dark satirical humor the shortcomings of an estranging urban world.

THE FIELD OF BATTLE

Today I am going to describe the field
Of battle
Just as I saw it, once the fate
Of the men who fought was decided,
Many having fought till death,
Others
Till they remained living still.

There was no choice:
Whoever could, died,
And whoever couldn't die, kept on walking,
The trees snowed their slow fruit,
It was summer, winter, a full year
Or more perhaps: it was the whole
Of life
That vast day of combat.

The wind carried blood in the west,
The earth was ashes in the east,
All the north was
Blockaded
By bare barbed-wire nets and by shouts,
And only the south,
Just
The south,
Presented itself broad and free to our eyes.

But the south didn't exist:
Nor water, nor light, nor shadow, nor ashes
Filled its void, its deep emptiness:
The south was a huge gulf,
An endless abyss from which,
Slowly,
The mighty vultures rose.

Nobody listened to the voice of the captain
For the captain didn't speak either.
Nobody buried the dead.
Nobody said:
"Give this to my girl friend if you meet her
Some day."

Somebody merely finished off a horse
That, with belly open,
In its death throes,
Filled the shadowy air with its terror:
The air which the night threatened.

Motionless, pinned to the hard
Earth,
Caught between panic and nothingness,
The men waited for the final
Moment,
Without resisting now,
Without defiance.

Some of them died,
As I said,
And the rest, lying down, prostrate,
Pinned to the earth in peace at last,
Waited
For I don't know what now—
Perhaps for somebody to tell them:
"Friends, you can go, the struggle . . ."

Meanwhile,
It is summer again,
And the wheat is growing
In what was a broad field of battle.

MESSAGE TO THE STATUES

You, stones
Violently deformed,
Broken
By the exacting blow of the chisel,
Will still show throughout the centuries
The last profile they left you:
Breasts unmoved by a sigh,
Firm
Legs ignorant of fatigue,
Muscles
Tense
In their useless effort,
Locks which no wind
Dishevels,
Open eyes that reject the light.
But
Your immobile
Arrogance, your cold
Beauty,
The scornful faith of unchangeable
Gestures, will one day
End.
Time is more tenacious.
The earth is waiting
For you as well.
You will collapse from your weight,
And you will be,
If not ashes,
Ruins,
Dust, and your
Dreamed-of eternity will be nothing.
To the stone you will return as stone,
Indifferent mineral, fallen
Rubble,
After having lived the hard, illustrious
Solemn, victorious, equestrian dream
Of a glory erected to the memory
Of something also dissolved in forgetfulness.

ELECTED BY ACCLAMATION

Yes, it was a misunderstanding.
                                 They shouted: "To ballots!"
And he understood: "To battle!"—he said later.
He was honorable and he killed a lot.
With pistols, with rifles, with decrees.

When he sheathed his sword he said, he says:
"Democracy is perfection."
The public applauded. Only the dead
Were silent and unmoved.

"The people's will shall be fulfilled.
From this moment on I am—[silence]—
The Chief, if you wish. Those opposed
May raise a finger."

The motionless majority of corpses
Gave him total command of the cemetery.

11 P.M. ADDRESS

Perfect citizens at this time,
Honorable heads of family
Who carry your napkins to your lips
Before uttering ritual words
As an act of thanks for the abundant meal:
Your responsibility as solid pillars
Of Western Civilization,
For the consumption of sodium bicarbonate
And for the paternalism that leads to servitude,
Demands on your part
A certain ignorance of facts also certain,
A final effort on behalf of everyone,
The stubborn unawareness of some realities,
The most meritorious faith, in short,
Which consists
Of not believing in the obvious.

I could swear that the earth stands still—
I have sworn to it already in the past—
And that the sun goes around it;
I could deny that the blood circulates—
I shall keep on denying it if need be—
Through man's veins; I could
Burn alive anyone who says the opposite—
I am burning him now—.

It is not that matters which are an object
Of controversy may be important:
The important thing is the strict
Resolution in error.
So the old lies turn into
The stuff of faith,
And in this manner
Whoever dares to disagree with us
Must confront the charge of impiety.
With this,
And a good lemon harvest,
And the invaluable aid of our allies,
We can hope for some periods
Of peace like today's,
On a night
Similar to today's,
After a supper
The same as today's.

Just as always, then, pray with me:
More faith, much more faith.
                              For in a certain way,
What we didn't see grow with such strength
Invites us to deny what we are watching.

DEATH OF A MACHINE

Spilling screws,
With the connecting rods now lifeless,
It made a last effort to move
The cogwheels. The pulley beat
Like a dark artery, but it only
Conveyed a slight tremor to the turbines,
That slowly turned, horrified,
With the expression of eyes that cloud over.
Later, the old machine
Ponderously broke down,
Choking in its fall
The sharp death-rattle of the valves.

A soft halo of reddish-brown
Rust,
Of mingled rust, and corrosion, and verdigris,
Rose slowly from the remains—
Still trembling—toward the misty
Skylight,
Polarizing the entering rays
Like a benediction from on high.
Someone shouted:
                    "Miracle!"
                              bleeding,
"Miracle!"
          freeing himself
From the embrace of the twisted iron.

Later we knew that that artifact
Had expired—
The man hardly matters—
With an odor of junk. And we understood.

PUBLIC PARK WITH PRIVATE LEGS

for Gabriel Celaya

. . . And the girls walk along with their legs bare:
Why do they use them
For walking?
I mentally review
Convincing roles
For them—the legs—,
Let's say: situations
Most useful to the man
Who watches them
Slowly,
Whistling between his teeth
A song recovered
Barely
   —that's a role I never like . . .—
On the cliff of forgetfulness.
If one looks hard, one sees that all of them
Are beautiful: those that go by, carrying
Hair, voices, breasts,
Eyes, gestures, smiles,
Somewhere else;
Those that stay
Crossed,
Bent like branches beneath the weight
Of warm beauty, drooping
From the sweet abandon of seated bodies;
Long and slim ones;
Smooth and shiny ones; the ones covered
With light down, touched by the grace
Of light, honey-colored, edible
And appetizing as fresh fruit;
And also—above all—those that delay
Their heavy journey to the ankle
At the curved profile that marks
The childish, merry, innocent,
Thoughtless, white calves.
Thinking about it again, it hurts to look:

So much scattered grace, inaccessible,
Left behind in the midst of spring,
Overwhelms the heart of the unsettled
Spectator
Who feels the humiliating burn
Of renunciation,
And he curses in a low voice,
And leans on the railing of the lake,
And looks at the water,
And sees his own face,
And spits idly, while his eyes
Follow the circles that
His loneliness, his fear, his spittle,
Trace in the taut surface.

SHOPPING CENTER

If one light symbolizes hope,
Do many lights symbolize
Many hopes? Or perhaps
Despair—
          for those that believe
That only one is needed . . .

The starry pavement
Turns on, turns off, turns on
Shining stars.
Dynamos generate nebulas
Of flaring neon,
Two-phase asteroids,
Comets with their burning tails
Of fleeting bulbs
That cross, streak, trace
Tiny orbits,
Bright trajectories,
Signals of incandescent mercury
In the dim apogee of the afternoon.

Many are those called, but it is not easy
To interpret the signs.
                              The finger
Of Publicity,
With its twilight script,
Clears up many things,
Labels space, stains the air,
Defines galaxies, spreads
The dust of kilowatts in the streets.
Open daily until seven:
Fallen sky,
Eternity shattered within reach of you.

OTHER TIMES

I want to be in another place,
Better still in another skin,
And find out if one sees from there,
Through the windows of other eyes,
Life equally grotesque some afternoons.

I would really like to know
The caustic effect of time in other guts,
Test whether the past
Steeps the tissues with the same bitter juice,
If all the recollections in all the memories
Give off this odor
Of musty fruit and rotten jasmine.

I long to see myself
With the hard pupils of he who hates me most,
So that in this way scorn
May destroy the remains
Of everything that oblivion will never bury.

ECLOGUE

I was brought up in a religious community
That had some very intelligent nuns.
On Thursdays they showed up in the cloisters.
"Give me your little hand,"
                                    the visitors said,
Offering them chocolates and coins.
But they gave nothing: just the opposite,
They begged continually.

On Sunday they rang the bells.
It was lovely to watch them, so sleek,
Licking their caps when the March
Sun at midday threatened a storm.

There was one, above all, very much the huntress.
She chased the little girls beyond the mud walls
And brought them back caught by the hair
To the little feet of the Mother Superior.

In the evening they took a walk
Along a highway shaded with black poplars.
They passed carts and flocks,
They walked along briskly, and the wind
Lifted the murmur
Of their voices and carried it
Flying through the fields
Among sheepbells and bees
Like a soft Gregorian bleating.
If they heard far off the blast of a car horn,
They scattered toward the ditches,
Noisy, excited and confused.
When the air
Was free of dust and racket,
One could see them, peaceful at last,
Pecking at blackberries in the bushes.

At the hour of the Angelus,
Tired and obedient,
They themselves returned to the cells,
As if the omnipresent hand of their Lord—
Tugging gently and firmly—
Led them by their rosaries.

NOTES ON CONTRIBUTORS

WALTER ABISH is a frequent contributor to the New Directions anthologies, his fiction having been included in *ND23, 25,* and *27.* His first novel, *Alphabetical Africa,* is scheduled for publication this year.

Biographical information on RYUNOSUKE AKUTAGAWA will be found in the note preceding his autobiographical novella, "Cogwheels." CID CORMAN edits and publishes the international literary magazine *Origin,* and his co-translator, SUSUMU KAMAIKE, teaches English at Doshisha University in Kyoto. Their English versions of Bashō's *Back Roads to Far Towns* and Shimpei Kusano's *Frogs & Others* were published by Mushinsha/Grossman. They recently finished six years' work on selections from the *Manyōshū;* over two hundred poems from the great ancient Japanese anthology, to be called *Old Songs for New,* will be brought out this year by Mushinsha.

FREDERICK BUSCH's novel *I Wanted a Year without Fall* was published in England in 1971, and a collection of stories, *Breathing Trouble,* in 1973. Syracuse University brought out his study, *Hawkes: A Guide to His Fictions.* He teaches literature at Colgate University and has recently completed a new novel, *Manual Labor.*

"Kayanerenhkowa" is a passage from the Nicaraguan poet ERNESTO CARDENAL's long poem *Homage to the American Indians,* published last year by The Johns Hopkins University Press in a translation by CARLOS and MONIQUE ALTSCHUL. Cardenal, the "revolutionary priest" who was for two years a Cistercian novice under the late Thomas Merton at the Monastery of Gethsemani, in Kentucky, wrote the "Coplas on the Death of Merton" included in *ND25,* translated by Kenneth Rexroth and Mireya Jaimes-Freyre. Merton himself contributed his own renderings of Cardenal's earlier work to *ND17* and to his *Emblems of a Season of Fury.* Donald D. Walsh's translation of *In Cuba,* Cardenal's penetrating observations of life under Fidel Castro's government, will soon be brought out by New Directions.

Born in Kentucky, COLEMAN DOWELL now makes his home in New York City and, in the warmer months, on Shelter Island. His novel *Mrs. October Was Here* is being published this spring by New Directions. An earlier work, *One of the Children Is Crying*, was brought out in 1968 by Random House, and his play *The Eve of the Green Grass* has been produced at the Chelsea Art Theatre.

WILLIAM EVERSON's "Tendril in the Mesh" was published in a limited edition in 1973 by Cayucos Books (1975 Cole Road, Aromas, California 95004) and is included in his new collection, *Man-Fate*. New Directions first brought out Everson's *The Residual Years* in 1948, shortly before the poet's conversion to Catholicism and entrance into the Dominican order, and an enlarged edition of the same work in 1968. In subsequent years, as BROTHER ANTONINUS, he became one of the most eminent figures in the revival of Catholic poetry. Not long ago, however, he renounced his vows and married, and now teaches at Kresge College, the University of California at Santa Cruz.

Biographical information on ANGEL GONZÁLEZ will be found in the note preceding his "Nine Poems." His translator, LOUIS M. BOURNE, was born in Richmond, Virginia, in 1942, and spent his childhood in the Himalayan foothills and in Cairo. He later attended the University of North Carolina, Hollins College (Virginia), and Corpus Christi College, Oxford. A former editor of *The Carolina Quarterly*, he has spent the last several years in Madrid, teaching English and translating Spanish poetry. His renderings of poems by Carlos Bousoño and Claudio Rodríguez appeared in *ND24* and *26*.

FREDERICK MORGAN is the editor of *The Hudson Review*. His collection of poems, *A Book of Change* (Scribner's), was a National Book Award nominee for 1973. Heinrich Cornelius Agrippa von Nettesheim (1486–1535) was a German cabalistic philosopher born in Cologne.

Ever since his first collection of fiction, *Color of Darkness* (New Directions, 1957), won him critical acclaim, JAMES PURDY has been a strong presence on the literary scene. His other works in print include *Malcolm* (Farrar, Straus & Giroux, 1959), *The Nephew*

(Farrar, Straus & Giroux, 1960), *Children Is All* (New Directions, 1962), *Cabot Wright Begins* (Farrar, Straus & Giroux, 1964), *Eustace Chisholm and the Works* (Farrar, Straus & Giroux, 1967), *Jeremy's Version* (Doubleday, 1970), and *I Am Elijah Thrush* (Doubleday, 1972).

The Objectivist poet CARL RAKOSI's most recent collections are *Ere-Voice* (1971) and *Amulet* (1967), both available from New Directions. He was awarded a fellowship in 1972 from The National Endowment for the Arts and last year was on the faculty of the National Poetry Festival held at Thomas Jefferson College (Michigan).

JEROME ROTHENBERG's fourteenth book of poems, *Poland / 1931,* will be published in the near future by New Directions. Along with his poetry and translations, he has edited several innovative anthologies as part of "an ongoing attempt to reinterpret the poetic past from the point of view of the present"; these include *Technicians of the Sacred* (Doubleday, 1968), *Shaking the Pumpkin* (Doubleday, 1972), and more recently, *Revolution of the Word: A New Gathering of Avant-Garde Poetry 1914–1945* (Continuum Books) and *America a Prophecy: A New Reading of American Poetry from Pre-Columbian Times to the Present* (Random House). A selection of his verse, *Poems for the Game of Silence,* appeared in 1971, and he currently edits, with Dennis Tedlock, the first magazine devoted to ethnopoetics, *Alcheringa.*

Born in Milan in 1930, ROBERTO SANESI has written several volumes of poetry. His "Three Poems" are taken from *Esperimenti sul metodo* ("Experiments on Method"). A limited bilingual edition of his work, *Angels Disturb Me,* was published in Italy in 1969 by Giorgio Upiglio, with English versions by WILLIAM ALEXANDER, who teaches at the University of Michigan.

The oldest daughter of immigrant parents, FAYE SOBKOWSKY was born in St. Louis, Missouri, in 1950. She was graduated last year from the City College of the City University of New York, where as a junior she participated in a writing workshop conducted by John Hawkes.

PAUL WEST has published seven novels, most recently *I'm Expecting to Live Quite Soon, Caliban's Filibuster, Colonel Mint,* and *Bela Lugosi's White Christmas.* "Brain Cell 9,999,999,999" is one of several short fictions he is collecting for a new book. His work has appeared in numerous periodicals, and he is currently with the English Department at Pennsylvania State University.

NEW BOOKS BY CONTRIBUTORS

Spring 1974

ALPHABETICAL AFRICA / Walter Abish. A delightful first novel, high comedy set in an imaginary dark continent that expands and contracts with ineluctable precision as one by one the author adds the letters of the alphabet to his book, and then subtracts them. While the "geoglyphic" African landscape forms and crumbles, it is, among other things, attacked by an army of driver ants, invaded by Zanzibar, painted orange by the transvestite Queen Quat of Tanzania, and becomes a hunting ground for a pair of murderous jewel thieves tracking down their nymphomaniac moll. Available Clothbound and as New Directions Paperbook 375.

MRS. OCTOBER WAS HERE / Coleman Dowell. A satirical American fantasy, like some of our dreams, both comic and frightening. Dowell's novel takes place in stagnant "Tasmania, Ohio." Upon this quintessential American town, Mrs. October—a lady of vast wealth whose hobby is revolution—descends with her mysterious entourage to stage her last great experiment. Available clothbound and as NDP368.

MAN-FATE: THE SWAN SONG OF BROTHER ANTONINUS / *William Everson.* The poet's first collection of verse since leaving the Dominican Order in 1969. Everson, who as Brother Antoninus was known for twenty years as one of the foremost Catholic poets of our time, describes the book as "a love poem sequence, a cycle of renewal, but it also concerns the monastic life, from the point of view of one who has renounced it. The love of woman and the love of solitude have contested together, and solitude has lost." Available clothbound and as NDP369.

In Preparation

MANUAL LABOR / Frederick Busch. A haunting novel concerning the collapse and renewal of a modern marriage. Set in rural New England, a man and a woman—each in a special way emotionally and physically damaged—are driven to find an equilibrium by rebuilding an ancient Maine farmhouse that becomes a paradigm of their very existence.

IN CUBA / Ernesto Cardenal. An incisive, wide-ranging account of life in a revolutionary society, subtitled "Report by a Marxist Monk." Translated for the first time from the original Spanish by Donald D. Walsh.

POLAND / Jerome Rothenberg. A collection of poetry evoking the Jewish immigration from Eastern Europe to America. Drawing from the kabbala and Hasidic lore, folk custom and historic fact, Rothenberg constructs a free-verse collage that gives voice to the interior journey from the Old World to the New.